Birthless

*When two close kindred meet,
What better than to call a dance?*

William Butler Yeats

Birthless

A Tale of Family Lost & Found

Maureen K. Wlodarczyk

Copyright © 2016 Maureen K. Wlodarczyk

All rights reserved.

ISBN-10: 1530316200
ISBN-13: 978-1530316205

This book may not be reproduced, transmitted, or stored in whole or in part by any means, including graphic, electronic, or mechanical without the express written consent of the author or publisher except in the case of brief quotations embodied in critical articles and reviews. This book is a work of fiction. Names, characters, places and incidents are either the product of the author's imagination or used fictitiously, and any resemblance to actual persons, living or dead, events or places is purely coincidental. References to actual persons or places are used strictly as setting and imply no involvement in fictional events.

Also by Maureen Wlodarczyk:
(www.past-forward.com)

Scarlet Letter Lives

Past-Forward:
A Three-Decade and Three-Thousand-Mile Journey Home

Young & Wicked:
The Death of a Wayward Girl

Canary in a Cage:
The Smith-Bennett Murder Case

Jersey! Then . . . Again

"A woman's heart is a deep ocean of secrets."

Gloria Stuart in *Titanic*

Contents

Introduction   i

Part One: Nicola

1. Bits & Pieces   1
2. Humpty Dumpty   7
3. The Old Folks Home   12
4. Misery Loves Company   17
5. Birds of a Feather   24
6. The Battle of Wounded Knee   29

Part Two: Caitriona

7. Photo Finish   34
8. Constructing a Future   38
9. Mind Games   43
10. Our Mutual Friend Tess   49

Part Three: Nicola

11. Who Do You Think You Are?	54
12. The Elder Orphans Club	58
13. Sometimes I Feel Like a Motherless Child	63

Part Four: Caitriona & Ellen

14. Trading Places	71
15. Mary Ellen Stuart	76
16. Ellen McNally	82
17. God Bless the Child	88
18. For Every Bad	94
19. The Proof is in the Pudding	100
20. Knock, Knock, Who's There?	105
21. Parting is Such Sweet Sorrow	112

Part Five: Caitriona

22. Redeeming Green Stamps	118
23. The Case of the Premonitory Priest	127
24. Follow the Yellow Brick Road	133

Part Six: Nicola

25. The Third Leg of the Stool	144
26. A Night Without a Morning	149
27. What Child is This?	156

Part Seven: Caitriona

28. There's More Where That Came From	164
29. In League with the 'Boy General'	170
30. Escape from New York	176
31. Where the High and Low Roads Meet	180
32. Grave Revelations	186
33. For Auld Lang Syne	191

Part Eight: Nicola

34. High-Flying	197
35. The Tell-All	203
36. Home to Tyrone	207
37. May the Road Rise Up to Meet You	213
38. My Brother's Keeper	217
39. Grave Revelations . . . Again	225

40. Pictures & a Thousand More Words	231
41. Family Reunions	236
42. Mid-Century Meanderings	243
43. Frozen in Time	251

Epilogue: Nicola   257

Introduction

Years ago, as I was having lunch with a group of women I worked with, the subject of old age came up. I no longer have any recollection of how that topic became lunch conversation. Perhaps someone at the table was dealing with an eldercare situation or the recent death of an older family member. Since some of the women were divorced and others had never married, I suspect that influenced the direction of the discussion. What I do remember, clear as day, is what one of them suggested:

"You know what we should do?" she said. "We should all live together when we're old. We could get a big house and take care of each other."

Although there was some tongue-in-cheekiness in the conversation, the overall consensus was that the idea of female communal living in our golden years had possibilities. The very fact that I remember the discussion proves it had some resonance.

Psychologists and researchers have studied the differences between male friendships and female friendships, generally concluding that friendships between men were 'side-to-side,' meaning that the men conducted their friendships by sharing activities like going to a sporting event. They were together to do something and their conversations were about what they were doing together or some related tangent.

The observations of women friends showed something quite different (but not surprising to women). Women's friendships were characterized as 'face-to-face' interactions, their bonding resulting from sharing information about themselves, their feelings, and other personal aspects of their lives. Said another way, women's friendships involve an intimacy that arises from sharing on a very personal level.

More than once, eating in a restaurant and hearing laughter, I have turned to see a group of women sharing a meal. It's a particular kind of laughter that signals long acquaintances, shared experiences, and lots of inside jokes. I myself rarely laugh harder than when I am with a group of female friends and we are retelling an old story for what seems like the hundredth time. It never gets old and neither does the gift of friendship. In fact, true friendship ages like fine wine, more flavorful and fortifying with time.

Birthless is the story of three 'mature' women, two in their 60s and one in her (very) late 70s, each of their lives altered by a long-concealed secret. Their acquaintance is transformed and forged into a friendship when each decides to share her secret. The bond of friendship sustains them as they face their pasts, searching for answers and hoping for closure. It is a story that is most definitely about 'face-to-face' relationships, sharing heart and soul, and facing up to one's ghosts with the support of friends.

Part One:

Nicola

1. Bits & Pieces

I threw open the car door and, in my panic, almost fell on my ass on the icy street. Hands on the car hood for balance, I made my way around to the curb. I had seen her hit the sidewalk as I drove up. She went down in a forward motion, looking very much like a baseball player diving into the bag at first base.

"Cat, I'm here. Are you all right?" I asked breathlessly.

She tried to lift her head but quickly lowered it again and answered in one word: "Shit!"

I called 911 on my cell phone and knelt down next to her looking for signs of bleeding. Her hands and knees were scraped and raw reminding me of the skinned knees and elbows that were a regular thing when we were growing up decades ago. If only now, so much older and more 'brittle,' we could still shake off a spill with some mercurochrome, a Band-Aid, and a scab that would fall off in short order (if we didn't pull it off ourselves first).

She turned her head slightly in my direction when I told her an ambulance was coming and a thick gush of bright red blood came from her nose. For a few seconds I thought I might scream or even pass out but instead, somehow, I was suddenly strangely calm. I put my face close to hers, held her hand and whispered that she would be alright and help was coming.

The EMTs, truly God's angels of mercy, arrived in just a few minutes despite the treacherous roads and no doubt multiplying calls for help from all over the area. They put a collar on Cat, stabilized her and slipped a hard board under her before lifting her up and into the ambulance. I followed them to the hospital in my car and sat in the ER grinding my teeth and doing that bouncing leg thing I do unconsciously whenever I have to sit still and I'm agitated, excited, or just have 'ants in my pants' for no reason.

Apparently I had a good size smear of Cat's blood streaked across my cheek, that being pointed out to me by a nurse who thought I was injured and in need of treatment as well. I made a quick trip to the ladies room and washed my face. Looking in the mirror I winced. Under the harsh fluorescent lighting and with my disheveled hair and now makeup-free face, I suddenly looked so old. Jesus, could this night get any worse?

Mercifully, I had no time to ponder on that or the lines on my face. I was told Cat was in good hands, remained conscious, and that it would be some time before I could see her. What they needed was for me to go to the admitting office to provide Cat's personal information. It was only when they asked about her medical insurance that I realized I had been carrying both her handbag and mine slung across my shoulder. As I sat next to the admitting clerk, a young woman with a petite gold ring through her nostril and a silver-studded leather bracelet that looked like a dog collar, I rooted through Cat's large leather satchel pulling out a dizzying assortment of contents. Keys, hand sanitizer, salt spray (for her much complained about 'sinus trouble'), Chapstick, make-up bag, vent brush, glasses, wallet and separate credit card case, phone, and my personal favorite, a pair of clean beige underpants in a Ziploc bag. I found her medical card in the credit card case and handed it over to the clerk. I did my best to answer what seemed an endless barrage of questions about everything from medicine allergies to menopause.

Once finished playing twenty questions, I headed back to the ER to ask about Cat's status. What greeted me in the waiting room was an entirely different scene from the one I had left about forty-five minutes earlier. While there had been relative calm and order then, the place was jumping when I got back. Stretchers were parked all over the waiting area, EMTs were jockeying for position, and every seat was taken. By the look of the place, the icy roads and sidewalks had taken their toll.

After a minute or two of scanning the chaos, I saw the familiar face of the nurse who had directed me to go to the admitting office as she trotted through the waiting area calling out someone's name. I wove my way through the clusters of people and caught up with her as she was directing some other patient's family to go to admitting. I gently touched her arm and asked about Cat. "Still being evaluated, it's going to be awhile" was her response.

I stood, propped up against a wall in the corner of the ER until a chair opened up and I all but dropped into it. Emergency rooms exist in a time warp where the minute hands on wall clocks seem to move imperceptibly like the 'watched pot' that will not boil. My eyes surrendered at about one in the morning, the wall clock winning our staring contest, and my head lolled back against the wall. The persistent din of voices, the sound of squeaking gurney wheels and the whirr of opening and closing automatic doors were unequal to the fatigue that had come over me. When I awoke to a nurse calling my name, it was after two and, not surprisingly, my eyes shot open before my mind engaged and momentary disorientation set in. A look around the room followed by a shot of pain in my stiff neck brought me back to reality. The crowd had thinned but the place was still a buzzing hive of activity.

I scanned the area looking for the nurse I had talked with earlier and spotted her across the room. I approached her and before I could speak she told me the 'wet' x-rays had just been read and showed a badly broken right patella, sprained left wrist . . . and a fractured nose. I cringed at the thought of a broken kneecap as my mind called up vignettes from mob movies with images of 'rats' tied in chairs as baseball bats delivered the penalty for their betrayals. I was quickly called back from my reverie when I heard the nurse say that Cat would need surgery as soon as possible to repair the shattered pieces of her kneecap. I asked what was entailed in that surgery and the words *wire and screws* were enough to make my empty stomach roll over.

Nurse Boland (I made it a point to check out her name badge) went on to say Cat was sedated for pain and her right leg had been set in a stiff cast from groin to ankle in order to ensure immobilization of her broken kneecap. She suggested I go home for a few hours and come back at ten o'clock to see Cat before her surgery which was tentatively scheduled for noon. Apparently, the attending doctors in the ER had already contacted Cat's GP and coordinated the selection of an orthopedic surgeon for the kneecap repair procedure.

I gave Nurse Boland Cat's phone thinking she would be looking for it when she woke up. As I turned to leave, Nurse Boland asked me if I was 'family' or 'next of kin' or if there was someone else who should be notified of Cat's condition and pending surgery. I parted my lips and, in consideration of the demands on her time, groped for an economy of words that would answer her question sufficiently if incompletely. I managed to respond with less than thirty words in true Twitter-worthy style:

"Caitríona has no living relatives that I know of nor do I. I am her closest friend and we are each other's emergency contact."

As I drove home, I wondered why I had included the fact that *I* have no living relatives in answering Nurse Boland's question about Cat's next of kin. Fortunately, I was so exhausted that I didn't have the strength for any annoying self-analysis on that point.

2. Humpty Dumpty

It seemed like only minutes after my head hit the pillow when the alarm went off. My eyes flew open as my brain tried to engage and my fingers groped for the alarm button. Silence restored, I tried to focus. The events of the prior evening came flooding back leaving no question that Cat's accident and the aftermath at the hospital were no dream. I rubbed my bleary eyes, sat up, and dangled my legs off the side of the bed. Since passing out some months earlier after abruptly popping out of bed, I had (at the recommendation of my 90-year-old neighbor) instituted a brief 'equilibrium pause' prior to exiting bed. My instincts told me this was not a day to blow that off.

A quick shower, a much-needed cup of tea, seven vitamins, and a 90-calorie cup of chocolate pudding and I was out the door. The temperature had risen and the icy glaze that wreaked havoc the night before had been reduced to scattered shallow pools of harmless liquid.

In twenty minutes I was in the revolving door entering the hospital. Cat had been moved upstairs from the ER and was in a semi-private room on the orthopedic ward. I peeked through the curtain separating her from her roommate and saw her, wide awake and absorbed in reading something on her phone. She had the beginning of a lovely pair of black eyes to go with her bruised nose.

"Something interesting?" I asked.

"They told me that since my nose isn't crooked and the fracture is relatively minor, there's no need to tape or splint it. I was getting a second opinion from my friends at WebMD and the Mayo Clinic on-line. Looks like it's true."

I tried not to smirk . . . with no success. "So, two hours away from reconstructive surgery on your smashed knee, the essential mechanism for walking and every other aspect of human mobility, you're busy making sure your nose is straight?" I asked.

"Damn straight . . . pun intended," she shot back. "You know what they say: when things hurtle out of control, people will focus their energy on controlling what they can."

"Cat, your nose looks fine but, in case you haven't noticed, you're sprouting a pair of black eyes and, by tomorrow, I'll be serenading you with my own rendition of *Rocky Raccoon*."

Now it was her turn to smirk. "That song isn't about a raccoon, my friend. You can google that while I'm under the knife."

The banter-fest ended when a nurse came in. She handed Cat a form that turned out to be an 'advance directive' (better known as a 'living will'). It could be filled out on the spot should Cat want to do so before her surgery. I didn't know if the nurse had brought it because it had already been discussed and Cat wanted it or if it was a standard procedure to offer the form. My question was answered when Cat picked up a pen and began filling out the form.

"I figured I better do this," she said, "assuming you're willing to be the person I appoint to make health decisions for me if I'm out of it."

"I'll do it for you," I said, "if you do it for me. I'll get another form from that nurse and we'll do both of them right now."

Cat couldn't resist one more snappy retort. "I guess that means two things: you expect me to wake up after the knee surgery . . . and you're not afraid of having a 'gimp' for your healthcare proxy."

Over my shoulder, as I exited the room, I fired the final salvo accompanied by a snarky smile and wink. "Well Rocky, what other choices do I have?"

The forms were quickly filled out and witnessed by one of the nurses and we were summarily promoted from being each other's emergency contacts to the significantly more dicey and daunting role of life or death monitor. I was asked to step out of the room so the anesthesiologist could talk with Cat in preparation for her surgery. Pre-op procedures followed and Cat was soon being wheeled out. I gave her a quick peck on the cheek and told her I would be waiting for her and would see her when she woke up.

As I gathered up Cat's few personal items and put them in a plastic bag, a voice from the bed next to Cat's called out to me. I pulled the curtain back in response and saw a young woman of about thirty with short black hair with pink streaks. She smiled and lifted a vividly-tattooed arm in greeting. I returned the smile, trying not to stare at the tattoos although I was itching to check them out as a means of sizing her up.

"Did your friend smash her kneecap?" she asked. "I shattered mine pretty good . . . motorbike wipeout. No, that's not true. I slipped and fell in the produce aisle of the damn supermarket. I wish I did do it on a motorbike. Sounds so much better than slipping on a soggy lettuce leaf."

I grinned and confirmed that Cat had indeed *smashed* her kneecap, leaving it in several puzzle pieces and in need of reconstruction asap.

"I have a history of dislocating my kneecap . . . started with a fall out of a tree when I was seven," she said. "When I took a flier on that wet lettuce leaf, I thought it was just another excruciatingly painful dislocation and, having shoved it back in on my own in the past, I grabbed my knee, gritted my teeth . . . and stopped dead. When I gripped the knee it felt like a handful of broken egg shell and I knew it was no simple dislocation. That's when I screamed for someone to call 911."

"Sounds awful," I said as I beat a hasty retreat from the room feeling like that 90-calorie cup of pudding was not long for my stomach as images of shards of egg shell flashed through my mind. Instead of Rocky Raccoon, maybe Humpty Dumpty would be a more fitting alias for Cat.

3. The Old Folks Home

Cat, in a 'piss and vinegar' mood I immediately recognized, all but hurtled into her hospital room following her last post-surgery physical therapy session, the objective having been to train her to maneuver on her dandy new crutches. She pitched forward through the doorway, did a graceless version of a pirouette, and landed safely on the bed.

"Now that you have your learner's permit for those nifty new sticks of yours, I guess we will commence with the frustrating process of getting you discharged, eh?" I asked with a smirk.

Cat glared and grinned at the same time. "Yes Nic, let's get the hell out of this place. I can't wait to check in for my stay at Sunrise. What a name for a damn nursing home, a place where the sun is *setting* on people's lives hour-by-hour, day-by-day."

Sunrise Continuing Care Home, more accurately described as a combination assisted living, skilled nursing, and rehabilitation facility, was the last place Cat wanted to stay while doing rehab for her battered knee but it was the most convenient and, compatible with her insurance, the obvious choice. Unfortunately, Sunrise was also the place where Cat's Aunt Nora had lived in the waning days of her life as dementia ravaged her mind and withered her body.

Nora was Cat's mother Moira's sister. Moira had died when Cat was just eight years old and it was her never-married Aunt Nora (proper name *Honora*) who raised her from that point on. Cat had struggled with the decision not to care for her aunt at home during the last months of Nora's life as she descended into the rabbit hole that is Alzheimer's. Despite knowing that she couldn't provide the level of care Nora needed, that fact did little to assuage Cat's feelings of guilt. Nearly a year later, that guilt still lingered and would no doubt be aggravated by Cat's stay at Sunrise, the place Nora sometimes jokingly called *the old folks home*.

The first leg of Cat's exit from the hospital was uneventful. She was taken out to the sidewalk in a wheelchair while I pulled the car up to meet her there. I trotted out to my car carrying the two plastic bags that held Cat's personal items, discharge instructions, and prescriptions, tossing them onto the back seat. It occurred to me that I better push the passenger seat back as far as it would go so Cat would be able to get in. Her bum knee, in a thigh-to-ankle brace and capable of bending only minimally, would need a wide berth.

I pulled up to the entrance, opened the front passenger side door all the way and helped Cat stand up on her crutches. I saw the color starting to drain from her face as she wobbled unsteadily. Mercifully, the sidewalk was handicap-friendly, no curb to negotiate. As gently (but as quickly) as I could, I succeeded in getting Cat's butt onto the seat, her legs still to be swung into the car. Seeing the fatigue already written on her face, I asked her to lift her good leg (the left) and move it into the car while I lifted her right ankle and slowly got the other leg in. Crutches stowed in the trunk, I carefully closed the passenger door and scurried into the driver's seat. Thank God Sunrise was just minutes away.

I pulled up to the front door at Sunrise and called the reception desk for help. We were quickly met with another wheelchair and two aides who very smoothly helped Cat out of the car. I exhaled audibly, unclenched my teeth and only then asked Cat if she was 'ok.' She just dropped her eyelids and moved her head ever so slightly left to right. No, she sure as hell wasn't *ok*. Cat's single room was ready for her and, in minutes, she had been helped to undress and was tucked in bed.

"Cat, I'm going to let you rest. I'll be back tomorrow morning. I'm going to get you some sweats and draw-string pants with wide legs. Somehow I don't think your usual skinny jeans and stovepipe slacks will work with your new leg gear. I'll bring a pair of your slip-on canvas shoes and a pair of sneakers, some socks, pajamas, and anything else I can think of. Whatever else you need as the days go by, I'll get for you. You focus on getting that knee working again so you can get out of here. I'll take care of the rest."

"Nic, just bring me my tablet, will you? Oh shit, does this place even have wifi? I'll go insane if I don't have web access while I'm here."

I checked at the front desk and confirmed that wifi was available (for an extra fee). Not wanting her to wait until the following day, I drove over to Cat's and picked up her tablet and her phone charger. Tablet, charger, and wifi code in hand, I went back to give Cat the good news that her temporary prison had a connection to the outside world but found her asleep. Suddenly feeling very tired myself, I headed home.

As spent as I was, sleep did not come. In the dark of my bedroom my eyes were wide open and, in the way that insomniacs do, I only made sleep less likely by checking the bedside alarm clock every few minutes. I tried slow deep breathing to no effect, gave up and let my thoughts go wherever they would. My mind flashed back to the day a decade ago when I first crossed paths with Cat and the inauspicious start of what would ultimately become the most important friendship of my life. The fickle winds of sleep must have come over me at that point as the next thing I knew the alarm clock was blaring.

4. Misery Loves Company, Not Therapy

I hit the snooze button and lay in bed with the light of a new day bleeding through the window shade. I deliberately called back my wandering thoughts of several hours earlier that had been snuffed out by the onset of sleep. As I thought about the past I wondered where the years had gone. In my younger days when older family or friends asked that question I would roll my eyes. No more . . . not now that I was walking in their road-worn shoes with an awareness of the capriciousness of life born of bitter and sweet experiences.

In November 2005 when Cat and I met, each of us was, in today's vernacular, a 'hot mess.' In our cases, the 'hot' part was not about good looks. We were simmering in the heat of our bitterness and roasting in the flames of our grief. Anyone who came close risked being singed and, believe me, when Cat and I stumbled upon each other in the small and often raw world of our group therapy sessions, sparks flew and there were plenty of flare-ups before we found our equilibrium and formed a bond. I've often told Cat that she can take personal credit for some of the lines on my face. She, in turn, delights in showing me her gray roots and saying that I should be chipping in toward the cost of her monthly touch-ups.

Grief-Speaks, sponsored by area churches and hosted by the local Y, was the ironically-named support group where Cat and I happened upon one another. Yes, there were some participants for whom the opportunity (and encouragement) to share their feelings of loss was at least palliative, if not curative. Looking back, I think those were the people whose grief was a purer version of loss, a sea of sorrow. Exhausted from swimming against the waves of grief, they were ready to link hands with those who could lift them up and lead them to dry land.

Cat and I (and some others in the group) were something else. We were angry. The initial shock and sting of our losses had not evolved into a siege of emptiness that had us searching for a means of escape. Instead of a dark, nagging abyss, we had bellies lit with a fire fueled by guilt we could not acknowledge to anyone, least of all to a group of strangers.

The moderator of the group, a trained counselor who had apparently mastered her own grief over the loss of her young son to cerebral palsy, did her best to draw out all ten group participants. She clearly believed that *sharing* was key to moving forward. She had precious little success getting a few of us to embrace that approach, Cat being the single worst case. I can't say I was much better but at least my facial expression was neutral if not signaling engagement. Cat's expressions, on the other hand, ran the gamut from lips twisted with scorn to eye rolls accompanied by audibly exhaled sarcastic sighs. Pressed on one occasion to weigh in on a discussion about the danger of being isolated by grief, Cat opined that 'misery does love company,' that pronouncement being met with another audible sigh . . . from the moderator.

At this point, you should be wondering why Cat even bothered to join the therapy group or why she continued to show up for meetings. The simple answer is that she needed to remind herself there were others suffering like her. She was not weak or crazy. I used to think it was our version of the movie *The Breakfast Club*.

Over the months that Cat and I went to the support group meetings we sort of evolved into our own splinter group. We went for a cup of coffee (tea for her) after meetings and then met for lunch or dinner a few times. We exchanged emails and I noticed that it wasn't uncommon for Cat to shoot me an email at two in the morning (and I was awake to read it when it came in). I suspected that she, like me, was a night owl and a late riser and I was right. We commiserated about being outliers in that regard and entertained each other with the gamut of annoying things that had been said to us because, unlike most of those in our lives, we preferred to get up at nine and end our days after midnight. From that simple but fateful start a friendship was born. With time came trust and we slowly opened up and told each other the painful events that brought us to the therapy group. So, Cat had been right: misery does love company . . . therapy, not so much.

I told her about my husband Sam. Sam and I met in college. We married just two months after graduation. Marrying before one's wisdom teeth had erupted was common in those days. We had imagined a long and happy life with all the customary flourishes: children, house with a white picket fence, professional success and more. We did not foresee infertility, alcoholism, or cancer. We flirted with divorce more than once but retreated from some combination of love, commitment, or fear of the unknown. As the years went by and we aged, the lure of starting over with a clean slate lost its luster when compared to the risks that came with that decision. After years of distance and just 'going along,' Sam stopped drinking and we slowly found our way back to each other. I thought that, as we approached our 'golden' years, we would be happy again. Then Sam was diagnosed with colon cancer.

Sam loathed doctors, some of that the result of being told time and time again that he must stop drinking. He would never agree to have a colonoscopy even though colon cancer was 'in his family.' Unbelievably, within a year after he stopped drinking, his health began to deteriorate. Stomach trouble came first, followed by weight loss (that we attributed to his stomach discomfort and diminished appetite). No need to go through the whole chronology. A large malignant growth was discovered in Sam's colon. Immediate surgery was necessary. Sam survived the surgery (just). The good news was that the tumor was contained, no evidence of any spread to surrounding tissue. The bad news? Sam came home with an ostomy bag.

We asked about prospects for reversing the ostomy and were told it might be possible after a period of recovery of at least three months. Sam and I soldiered through the process of changing the ostomy bag. He tried to conceal his embarrassment and I tried to hold back my tears when I carefully cleaned the red, raw skin that ringed the ostomy opening. By trial and error we fell into a daily routine and, somehow, dealing with that accursed bag of fecal matter actually brought us closer together.

As the three-month anniversary of the surgery approached, Sam started planning for the reversal of his ostomy. He made an appointment with his surgeon and we went in for a discussion of the reversal process. The doctor explained both the prerequisites that would determine Sam's suitability for the reversal procedure and the surgical process . . . with much emphasis on the risks accompanying the surgery. Those warnings had no effect on Sam's desire for the surgery (nor mine for that matter). We asked how to move forward to have the reversal surgery. A battery of tests and more doctor visits followed and, finally, Sam's surgeon scheduled the procedure – nearly eight months after Sam's original cancer surgery.

When the surgery was over, I was given the good news that the reversal had been successful. Sam spent eight days in the hospital and was then transferred to a rehab facility so he could have professional nursing support and monitoring for an additional two weeks. He was discharged from the hospital and arrived at the rehab by ambulance at six in the evening. I arrived there about a half-hour after Sam.

As I approached his room, I heard anxious voices and saw several staff checking Sam's vitals. In admitting Sam, the nurses had observed that his skin was ashen and clammy to the touch and he was running a fever. They told me they were calling for transport to take him back to the hospital as quickly as possible. By eight o'clock Sam was in the ER. Two hours later I was told that the reversal was leaking and immediate surgery would be needed or he could die. That 'immediate' surgery didn't begin until two in the morning. Sam survived the surgery but saving him meant undoing the reversal and reconnecting the ostomy with no chance of repeating the reversal surgery in the future.

The ordeal left Sam devastated mentally and stripped of all his physical strength. He was eventually discharged from the hospital and went back to the rehab facility where, over a period of two months, he had two more crises that sent him back to the ER. He gave up. He had no more fight in him. He continued to decline.

I arranged for hospice care at our home and hoped that escaping the institutional environment for home care might make a difference. He lived for another month at home before dying, expertly and tenderly cared for by amazing hospice nurses and aides. During his last days as I lay in bed alone, my mind would replay our visit to the surgeon when we excitedly asked about the reversal surgery and how we could get it scheduled. The surgeon's words of warning about the risks came back to me. That was followed by the *if only* list, the first of those being 'if only we left well enough alone and accepted life with the original ostomy, Sam wouldn't be at death's door.' Of course, besides blaming myself, I blamed the surgeon who called the reversal procedure a success and then released Sam from the hospital with obvious symptoms that something was wrong. The icing on the cake was when I discovered that Sam had taken out a very large life insurance policy when he stopped drinking and I was, of course, the beneficiary. Once I stopped crying about that, I started looking for a grief support group.

5. Birds of a Feather

I was the first to share the events that brought me to the grief support group. Even after I put it all out there, Cat struggled with the decision to tell me why she joined the group. At first the story came out in short bursts and unconnected vignettes mostly about her husband Rick. They married when Cat was thirty-one and Rick was thirty-five . . . because Cat was pregnant and each of them wanted the child they had unintentionally conceived. My sense (early on) was that there was little or nothing meaningful connecting Cat and Rick except their love for that child, a daughter named Gemma.

Since Cat never talked about Gemma and there was no sign of her in Cat's life as I knew it, I jumped ahead to the conclusion that Gemma was likely dead. It took a great effort on Cat's part to say the painful words: "My daughter died in a car accident along with her father, an accident that I survived." Later on she told me the circumstances of the car accident that had instantly changed her life, stealing the central focus of her world.

Gemma was eighteen when the accident happened. She was an extremely intelligent young woman who had worked hard in school with the goal of being accepted to the journalism program at Villanova University. Not only was she accepted to that program, she was offered a scholarship grant as well. Rick and Cat were driving Gemma to Villanova when a car veered out of the opposite lane, struck their car and sent it careening into a ditch off the shoulder of the road. The car flipped over and Cat, who was not wearing a seatbelt, was thrown clear of the wreck. Gemma and Rick were trapped in the car which burst into flames, killing both of them as Cat lay yards away semi-conscious.

But there was more, that being the guilt that haunted Cat and eventually drove her to leave the house after weeks of living in her pajamas, struggling to find the motivation to wash her face and brush her teeth, rarely eating a decent meal and, window shades pulled down, sitting motionless for hours in a recliner staring off vacantly. The events of the minutes before the accident ran through her mind like a tape on an endless loop. Rick had missed the exit where they were supposed to get off the highway and Cat was chewing on him for not paying attention, that starting a volley of back and forth bickering between the two of them. Gemma, as she had so often done over the years, tried to intervene and defuse the situation. Her allergies were acting up and she began to cough as she pleaded with her parents to stop arguing. It was her coughing more than her pleading that stopped the argument. Cat reached into her purse and pulled out a package of cough drops and, undoing her seatbelt, turned toward Gemma in the back seat meaning to hand her the box. At just that moment, a large SUV traveling in the opposite direction suddenly veered into their lane.

There would be no exciting day setting up Gemma's new dorm room and meeting her roommate. In fact, not one more word would pass between Cat and her beloved daughter or her husband of eighteen years. While it was clear that Rick was in no way at fault for the accident, Cat was also plagued by 'what-ifs.' What if he had not missed the exit? What if she had not distracted him by bickering? Might he have seen the oncoming SUV and avoided it somehow? How could she live with the knowledge that Gemma's last words were uttered in an attempt to stop yet another of her parents' arguments?

Just as I had received a financial windfall after Sam's death, Cat received a significant accident settlement for both Gemma and Rick's deaths and for the injuries she sustained. So, there we were: birds of a feather, our wallets flush with blood money, our lives gutted, our bond built on a foundation of loss cemented with guilt.

I was jolted awake by the alarm going off again. Snooze time was over. A quick shower and cup of tea and I was off to see Cat at Sunrise. The days start early at Sunrise, at least it was early by

Cat's and my standards. By the time I got there, at a little after nine o'clock, she was already working with the physical therapist. She was scheduled for some one-on-one sessions with the therapist to work on her knee recovery along with some group sessions geared to residents with mobility issues. If you were ever clicking through the more obscure cable channels and caught one of those chair exercise shows for seniors, that's pretty much what the group sessions were like.

Cat resisted attending the group sessions at first but as boredom set in and the hours and days dragged by, she agreed to go if only to pass the time. She swore she would beat me with her crutch if I made any jokes about it but, keeping a safe distance, I teased her mercilessly and she dished it right back, both of us descending into fits of laughter.

"Tell me Cat," I once said, "with all that arm action and coordination in your group therapy sessions, when will the flock be ready for the flight back to Capistrano?"

Cat had responded in kind: "Capistrano, where'd you get that? We've been asked to be the new opening act for the Blue Angels. When the sun hits the sea of sequins on our outfits, it will be blinding! Do remember to wear your shades my dear."

Cat always had a soft spot for the elderly and a way of connecting with them. While her Aunt Nora was residing in the assisted living wing at Sunrise, Cat's visits were looked forward to not only by

Nora but also by her aunt's 'crew' of friends. A few of those ladies were still living at Sunrise and soon spotted Cat and asked her to 'hang out' with them during the daily afternoon happy hour. A little wine in a plastic cup, a little Sunrise gossip and, if Cat encouraged it enough, the sharing of their life stories. Cat was truly interested in the tales they told her, especially stories about their childhoods. She never tired of hearing about their lives during the Depression and World War II. She would ask them to tell her about their parents and grandparents, relishing stories about the days when family immigrants were making their way in a strange new world. Stories of economic struggles and ethnic or religious prejudice were routinely told without any flavor of bitterness. Instead, those aspects of their early lives were most often only an aside to recollections of the closeness, warmth, and happiness that came from the nurturing presence of family and neighbors.

One of Nora's crew, Miss Ellen McNally, was a favorite of Cat's. She sat next to Cat at the group exercise sessions and was the main instigator in getting Cat to be a regular at happy hour. It would turn out that Ellen and Cat's reconnection had the makings of a seismic (or karmic) event in Ellen's life. There's an old Irish saying: *Faigheann iarraidh, iarraidh eile* which roughly translates as *the search for one thing finds another thing*. You can say that again (assuming you can pronounce it).

6. The Battle of Wounded Knee

Cat earned every plastic cup of wine she downed at the daily Sunrise happy hours. After reading about the aftermath of patella fractures, hers being a more tricky comminuted fracture requiring repair using pins and wire, she was hell-bent on making sure she had the best possible recovery. Patella fractures constitute only one percent of all bone fractures and the necessary weeks of relative immobilization via cast and/or brace result in significant thigh muscle atrophy. In addition, victims of patella fractures often develop arthritis in the injured knee due to cartilage damage. Some have knee pain that never ends. Instead of being discouraged by the prognosis, Cat was motivated and determined to take charge of her recovery.

Cat worked diligently with the physical therapist and independently. Straight leg raises, walking on the treadmill, and working her legs with an exercise ball were just some of the activities aimed at strengthening the withered quad muscle and coaxing the repaired knee to bend once again. The therapist regularly measured the knee's range of motion, the goal being to get back to a near full natural bend. And then there was the scariest piece of exercise equipment: the stationary bike. The therapist instructed Cat to sit on the bike, put her feet on the pedals and then just rock the pedals back and forth as far as was comfortable. There was no expectation that her wounded knee was ready to do a full rotation of the pedals. That wasn't going to happen for weeks and, without dedication to the PT exercise regimen, it would essentially be impossible.

Sometimes I would work with Cat when she was doing the exercises and only when she sat on the bike did I see her tense. Knowing that her knee was incapable of bending enough to do even one rotation of the pedals was unnerving and, when she tried to push it to extend the range of pedaling, it was actually frightening. I was there the day the battle of the exercise bike was won. Cat was testing the limits of the pedaling motion when, suddenly, momentum took control and her knee lurched forward at the top of the rotation and a full spin resulted. I cheered and, looking up, saw a dumb-founded Cat, her cheeks drained of color with the thought that she might have reinjured her knee. Realizing her knee had finally surrendered and she had reached a new recovery benchmark, she would not get off the bike and showed off by pedaling a complete rotation forward and then backward.

I wasn't the only one who was proud of her. Word spread quickly among the Sunrise gang. When Cat entered the room for happy hour, she was met with a congratulatory banner and applause thanks to Ellen McNally's efforts. The first plastic cup of wine was raised in a toast to Cat. I brought over a large tray of shrimp and another of vegetables and dip, all of it devoured with gusto.

Later that afternoon, Cat and I went by Ellen's room to thank her for leading the celebration. Despite spending time with Ellen in the common areas, Cat had never seen Ellen's small efficiency unit. It was a compact but adequate L-shaped room with double closet and a tiny kitchenette (a few cabinets but no stove, only a microwave, sink, and mini-fridge) and enough space for her television and recliner. Her twin-size bed with brass headboard was positioned at the far end of the space along with a high chest. Next to her bed was a small nightstand with two shelves filled with books. It was a 'girly' room with a lace-trimmed floral bedspread (and matching pillow shams) and coordinating lace curtains that let the sunlight filter in through the double window. Framed watercolors that Ellen herself had painted many years before flanked each side of that window. It was a cheerful space that thoroughly suited Ellen.

As we were taking it all in and telling Ellen how nice her little apartment was, Cat suddenly walked across the room and picked up a book sitting on top of the nightstand and leafed through it.

"Ellen," Cat said, "are you reading *Tess of the d'Urbervilles*? It's my all-time favorite book . . . along with *The Scarlet Letter*. It's the exceptionally sensitive and intuitive way both Hardy and Hawthorne created such complex female heroines and wove the stories of their incredibly difficult lives. I've lost count of how many times I've read those two books but every time I do I discover something new that I didn't notice before."

"I couldn't have said it better myself," Ellen said with a smile. "Like you, I've read *Tess of the d'Urbervilles* a number of times, the first time when I was about seventeen. Reading it then, when I was about the same age as the character Tess, I guess I could relate to the story of a naive young woman victimized by family and left no choice but to go out on her own and try to survive. Anyway, after all these years, that book is just like an old friend I revisit time and time again."

Cat and I did wonder what Ellen meant when she said she could *relate* to the story of a naive young woman victimized by her family. As it turned out, anything we could have imagined wouldn't come close to the reality that caused Ellen to identify with Tess.

Part Two:

Caitriona

7. Photo Finish

Sometimes I sit and stare at the last photo I took of Gemma. She was sitting on the back bumper of our Subaru wagon among boxes and bags, some piled in the car, others on the ground waiting to squeeze their way in. Gemma's smile is radiant with the promise and possibilities of a young woman heading off to college and the start of an exciting new stage of her life. Just hours later the light in her large deep brown eyes would be snuffed out forever.

Sometimes that same photo is so painful for me to look at that I put it in a drawer to escape it. Then the longing for Gemma overtakes me and compels me to open the drawer. My fingers wrap around the framed image of my darling child . . . my beautiful girl. That photo is, all at once, a precious gift and a nettle embedded in the depths of my heart.

Weeks after the accident, a box arrived, sent by the Pennsylvania State Police. In it was my purse and the remnants of its contents including a battered Canon autofocus camera. The purse had been on my lap at the moment of the crash and was thrown clear of the wreck along with me. After opening the box, on impulse, I started heaving all its contents in the trash and, only after pitching the camera into the recycling bin, did it occur to me to see if the digital card was still in it. I pulled it out of the bin, opened the card compartment and was able to pop it out. It was undamaged. That was how I came to have that last photo of my Gemma.

For weeks after the accident I sat curled up in a fetal position in the leather recliner in our living room as scenes of the hours leading up to the crash cycled through my mind. Over and over, on a continuous loop, I relived that day. Once again I felt the tension between my joy at Gemma beginning her college adventure and my dread of how much I would miss her. She was the glue that made the three of us a family, the bridge between her father and me. Without her, there would only be Rick, me, and the canyon between us. Little did I know that I was destined for a loneliness so much more profound than marital estrangement.

Sometimes I wondered what would have happened if Rick had also survived the crash. Would we have become closer as a result of our mutual wrenching grief or would we have co-existed, each in our own personal hell? When I was in a mood to be mercilessly honest with myself I faced the fact that I would always have blamed him for Gemma's death. If he hadn't missed the exit, we would not have been in the path of the oncoming car that killed her.

Often, I wished I had died in accident . . . for different reasons depending on my self-pitying mindset. I should've died so I didn't have to live without Gemma, a punishment I did not deserve. I should've died in place of Gemma as she deserved to live so much more than I did. I should've died with Gemma but Rick should have lived, never able to forget that his wrong turn killed his child and her mother. At times I would pick apart those three death scenarios, expanding them as if I were constructing a script or screenplay. I would be drawn into the nuances of these imagined scenarios of my death in what was almost like a psychological self-examination. I noticed things, revelations that showed me my grief was impure, tainted with anger at Rick and regrets about a marriage that never should have been. When I imagined that Gemma and I both died and Rick survived to live a life knowing that 'his wrong turn killed his child and *her mother*,' why didn't I refer to myself as *his wife* rather than as Gemma's mother? I knew the answer.

After days and weeks of reruns of grief, anger, and regrets, refusing support from friends and my Aunt Nora, getting little decent sleep, eating a diet of crap (when I did eat) and hiding out in dark rooms with shades pulled down day and night, I was finally spent. I hadn't the physical or mental strength to continue the downward cycle I was on. I either had to finish myself off or get the hell up and go on with my life. I admit that it was a crap-shoot and I wasn't sure which way it would turn out at first. It sounds cliché but I couldn't handle the thought that if I offed myself and was reunited with Gemma in some afterlife, she would be ashamed and disappointed at my weakness and I would be the hypocrite who had preached to her about never giving up on life and then had done just that.

The struggle between digging in and moving on continued for a while, the battle being won in small increments like the lifting of window shades to allow the outside world in once again and the tedious reading of the pile of unopened mail on the kitchen table. From that came the need to pay a bill or respond to an expression of sympathy. Grungy sweats fell to the bathroom floor as hot showers were resumed. Then one day, like a daring agoraphobic, I opened the front door and stepped onto the porch, my lungs snapping to attention in the brisk autumn air and the pupils of my eyes in full retreat from the sudden assault of daylight. An immediate longing to see Aunt Nora followed. It was her embrace, devoid of any judgments and warm with unconditional love, that told me I would go on.

8. Constructing a Future

Aunt Nora, with exquisite tact, did suggest that I might continue my journey up from the ashes of my fractured life by participating in some form of therapy. Her reasoning was that, beyond her, I really had no close friends, no soul-baring confidants. While the idea of therapy repulsed me, I couldn't deny that I came up short when it came to a human support system.

I had worked from home for many years, a consultant in the book editing arena. Often, I never met the people I worked for or with. My professional reputation was excellent and assignments usually came to me via referrals so I didn't have to be a marketer, that being a very good thing. I had no natural sales skills and hated 'working' a room of strangers for any reason – professional marketing or personal schmoozing. I never felt the need to know our neighbors on the streets where we lived. Sometimes I almost proudly pronounced myself 'standoffish.' I now think a better description would be that I am somewhat insular and insecure. Hearing the word *insecure* used to describe me would no doubt provoke smirks from people who knew me personally or dealt with me professionally due to my inherent tendency to speak my mind, even to the point of combativeness or obstinacy. In my experience, having a personality that is orally-active and committed to its beliefs and principles (even if that commitment sometimes results in unpopularity) does not necessarily equate to being a confident person.

Aunt Nora was a reader, her bottomless store of intellectual curiosity seemingly without bounds. She devoured books on a gamut of topics from classic literature to science to 'new age' and self-help. It was she who introduced me to Jane Austen, the Brontes, Hawthorne, and my dear Thomas Hardy. She showed me the enormous world that lives in the pages of books, a world in which I have always felt at home. I counted Elizabeth Bennett, Hester Prynne, Cathy Earnshaw, and Tess D'Urberville my 'friends.' Perhaps I should add 'bookish' to my characterizations of myself. Until Gemma came along, I just was not engaged with the actual world around me. Her birth realigned the planets of my personal solar system.

In recommending therapy Aunt Nora quoted her favorite existential psychologist, Rollo May: "Depression is the inability to construct a future." Hard to argue with that succinct, pragmatic definition of the abyss that is depression – a deep dark hole with walls as cold and slick as ice, no ladder for escape to the light, and no way to respond to the sounds of possible rescuers in the distance – ergo, no conceivable future. Nora pointed out that despite all I had lost, I still had the inborn reservoir of tenacity that had on occasion severely deviled her when I was growing up. Her belief was that I needed to draw on that to propel myself forward with the help of others, even if it meant deviling them as well. We agreed that, for me, one-on-one therapy sessions were too personal and intrusive . . . and likely to turn into debates. With my 'standoffish' tendencies and need for demarcated personal space, a group therapy session was a better bet. In that venue I could retain some modicum of anonymity and assume an 'observer' role.

I listened patiently to Nora. (I owed her that.) I could feel the resistance bubbling up inside me and the 'fight or flight' signals coming on strong. After a series of delaying tactics and orchestrated episodes of procrastination, I surrendered. Nora handed me a list of three local therapy groups focusing on grief and loss. I admit I chose *Grief-Speaks* out of perversity as I had no intention of talking about my situation.

In November 2005, about three months after the crash that killed Gemma and Rick, I cruised into a *Grief-Speaks* group session, failed to sign in as required, and took a seat in back corner of the room. Minutes later a woman came in, obediently signed the roster sheet, scanned the room, and made her way to the rear without interacting with any of the others congregating in the front of the room. She was thin and angular, sort of bony, about five feet seven inches tall with graying light brown French-braided hair. She took off her well-worn leather jacket to reveal a squint-inducing tie-dyed polo with a pair of aviator sunglasses hanging on the neckline. Her jeans were neither 'boyfriend' nor 'skinny,' but they were supremely broken in and fit as if made for her. My eyes finished their top to bottom examination, ending on a pair of lace-up leather granny boots that had to be a survival from the days of Janis Joplin and Twiggy. She piqued my curiosity and I mused that she was just the kind of person one needed to partner with for a day of thrift shop adventures.

In the ongoing weeks of group meetings, the woman in the granny boots (Nicola) and I mostly remained on the fringes of both the room and the discussions. The group leader, Sandy, made a valiant effort to draw us into the dialogue and sharing . . . to no avail. Nicola was more sympathetic to Sandy's efforts and so gave some lip service. Looking back, I wish I had made a similar effort. Instead, according to Nicola, I offered up grimaces, smirks, and audible sighs along with at least one smart-ass response to a direct question from Sandy. It's a wonder that Nicola didn't get up and move her seat to the front of the room but, thank God, she didn't.

Nora had prodded me to go to therapy. Those discussions did nothing for my attitude or outlook. What therapy did do was bring me into Nicola's path and that unexpected event brought me my first real friend, a person whose presence in my life would be balm for my broken heart and a compass that helped me find my own 'true north.'

Thank you Nora.   Sorry Sandy.

9. Mind Games

Here I am at the 'old folks home,' hobbling around and looking not much different from the regular residents that call this place home. As an assisted living facility I guess it's not bad. The wrap-around porch, complete with rocking chairs, and the landscaped grounds are welcoming. The traditional décor and wallpapered and wainscoted walls do give the place a less institutional vibe. There's even a small ebony baby grand piano in the lobby that some of the residents periodically play for their pleasure and that of their fellow Sunrisers.

The rehab section of the facility offers services to both residents and non-residents like me who are recovering from accidents or surgery. The staff is pleasant enough and the food is passable with lots of sweet desserts. I have been told that the elderly gradually lose a good deal of their sense of taste. Judging from their enthusiasm in cleaning their desserts plates, I can only assume that our sweet tooth is the last of our taste buds to fail us. Better that than instead ending your life with only the ability to taste vegetables, especially creamed corn. No one who has jumped the hurdles that must be bested to reach their *golden years* should have to endure that.

I suppose I must mention the memory care wing at Sunrise. Yes, Sunrise offers continuing care for residents under assault from dementia or Alzheimer's who are no longer able to function independently at the assisted living level. Once a person walks or is pushed through the front door of the Sunrise Continuing Care Home, their exit comes with a death certificate as a rule. It pains and shames me to think about my Aunt Nora being an example of that seamless Sunrise end-of-life progression. I will never be able to convince myself that having her at Sunrise in the last terrible year of her life was a decision that was only motivated by her needs. No matter how many people tell me I could not have given her the 24/7 level of physical and mental care she needed at home, only I truly know how much she sacrificed in raising me and why I feel I didn't do enough for her.

It was originally Nora's idea that she move to an assisted living 'community.' She had a few friends who had moved to Sunrise and extolled its virtues including having meals prepared for you and served in the spacious dining room and having your wash done and returned to you the same day, neatly folded. Sunrise had its own minibus of course and there were regularly scheduled trips to local stores, outings for ice cream or other treats, and monthly rides to casinos in Atlantic City.

Nora lived at Sunrise for nearly two years without any problems but for a bout of the flu and some minor dust-ups with residents she spotted being unkind to someone or with staff members who were unresponsive to the entreaties of a resident clearly in need of attention. The staff called her the 'mayor' of the second floor which she took as a compliment. She was proud as a peacock when the facility manager asked for permission to bring touring guests (potential new residents and their families) to see her little efficiency apartment.

The bottom fell out so suddenly, without warning. She celebrated her 85th birthday in fine form but for the noticeable progression of her memory and other cognitive issues. We had a sheet cake that fed all the residents and on-duty staff and Nora relished being the center of attention. The photos I took on that last birthday show a celebratory day full of smiles, sweets, and gifts. Barely two weeks later, I received a call from the Sunrise manager and nursing director who asked to see me as soon as possible and said Nora had become combative and angry with residents and staff.

When I went over there, I found Nora in a very agitated state. She was abrupt and edgy with me and told me how one of her newer friends had tried to take *her* seat in the dining room. She said she 'would always hate' that woman, that kind of vitriol so unlike

Nora. Her mental state and personality were altered and nothing I said comforted or calmed her. It was the first day of the rest of her life, a life that would start with her being moved to the 'cottages' (translate that: secure memory care unit), followed by nearly a year of downward spiral, mental and physical, and a slow, cruel death so undeserved by her and heart-breaking for me. The diagnosis was Alzheimer's (or dementia). What the hell does the label matter anyway? I was helpless to relieve her suffering and could only be vigilant and visible as to her care, my involvement and advocacy ensuring there would be no lapse and nothing lacking in her treatment, medically or as an inmate in the Sunrise memory care unit. Unable to speak up for herself, I would be her voice.

Never knowing what version of my Nora I would find when I visited, I learned to be steady and adaptable. Some days she would be sleeping so deeply (often snoring) that I could not wake her so I would leave her at peace and just sit in her room. Other days she would be in the grip of anxiety, speaking a combination of parsed words and gibberish as her mind roiled. Infrequently she called me Kitty, the pet name she had for me as a child and my heart was warmed that she recognized me. She lost more and more weight despite the staff helping her eat and giving her protein shakes to augment her diet. Medication was prescribed and administered for her spinal stenosis pain and to take the edge off her anxiety.

After several months, Nora became a hospice patient due to her rapidly declining physical and mental situation. Over time her anxiety abated and she seemed less in the throes of whatever fear or anguish had been roiling her mind. Sometimes I would ask her if I could lay down next to her and 'rest.' She would softly say 'yes' and I would stroke her hair and talk about things we had done and people we knew. I would tell her I loved her and, a few times, when she said 'love you too,' I felt my heart leap. Not long before she passed away, she had been saying my mother's name and then something I could not make out, repeating it over and over. Then, clear as a bell, she said: "God is punishing me. When will He end it with me?"

Nora did not go quietly into the dark waters of dementia. She never became non-verbal as so many victims do. She held onto her remaining bits and pieces of reality with white knuckles like a person hanging from a window ledge high above the pavement, determined not to hurtle downward. To the end she seemed aware that her mind was taunting her and fought back in a futile struggle to right herself.

Medical professionals often say that the course and manifestations of Alzheimer's and dementia follow no predictable pattern or timeline, each case being unique to the patient. However true, that pronouncement offers nothing useful to those who are watching the devastating deconstruction of their loved ones. Groping for answers and trying to manage my fears and feelings as I watched Nora's decline, I sometimes wondered if victims who become non-verbal and seemingly placid suffered less than people like Nora who are buffeted back and forth between anguished imaginings and fleeting episodes of reality. Should I wish that she go silent, for her sake (and mine)? But what if those who no longer speak are trapped without a voice and cannot let us know that they too are being heaved to and fro as their own minds turn against them?

In a void of tangible information and meaningful answers to my questions there was one thing I did know. Rather than wishing for longevity, we would do better to wish we never live long enough to have our own minds turn against us and condemn us to such a cruel death. Rather than worrying about wrinkles and saving up for plastic surgery to turn back the hands of time, we had better focus on our brains. No amount of facelifts or Botox can tame an erratic, besieged brain nor will a cosmetically restored face lessen the ugly indignities of the journey that is death from Alzheimer's or dementia.

10. *Our Mutual Friend Tess*

Despite the fact that being at Sunrise resurrected painful memories of Nora's death, the rehab facilities were what I needed and rekindling acquaintances with Ellen and a few other former members of Nora's posse was actually pleasant. Those old girls, with their unfiltered opinions and unconstrained by today's political correctness, were a real hoot. They not only called out each other and those in their daily sphere, they kept up with the goings-on in the outside world. Their take on the faux celebrity Kardashians and others like them (think overexposed supermodels and misbehaving athletes du jour) was spot on . . . and hilarious. Two of them, having been school teachers, skewered the lapses in spelling and grammar in on-line news reports they saw on *Yahoo*, *Huffington Post* and other sites. Yes, these seventy and eighty-somethings surfed the web with a good deal of facility, googling all the way.

I thoroughly enjoyed spending time with them and often sat with them for the daily afternoon 'happy hour,' sipping wine from plastic cups and nibbling on snacks. Between that and the desserts served at both lunch and supper every day, I expected that when I checked out of Sunrise, the only skinny part of me was going to be my atrophied right thigh muscles. Not a pleasant prospect but it did little to stop me from indulging.

One afternoon, Nicola and I stopped by Ellen's apartment to thank her for organizing a celebration when I succeeded in getting my bum knee to make a complete rotation on the stationary exercise bike for the first time. It happened so unexpectedly that I gasped out loud thinking the kneecap would shatter once again. Judging from the way Nicola came charging toward me in response to the gasp and expression of panic on my face, I must have looked utterly petrified. In just seconds, realizing all was well with the knee, I began pedaling cycles both forward and backward with triumph. A celebration was most certainly in order and Ellen wasted no time getting it arranged.

Ellen's place was neat and tasteful even if more frilly than I would choose. The florals and lace, brass headboard, and traditional cherry-toned wood furniture suited her. Lots of books, no surprise considering she was a retired librarian. Something still seemed missing or a bit impersonal despite the lovely décor. Although the walls were decorated with some lovely prints and original watercolors painted by Ellen herself, there were no family photos on display. I recalled Nora telling me Ellen had never married and was a 'spinster librarian.' Ellen's delicate features were still attractive to the eye and I couldn't imagine she had never been courted or proposed to over the years.

As my mind wandered and my eyes scanned the room I walked closer to Ellen's bookshelves. I recognized many of the classic titles and noticed, from the bindings, that the copies were old ones, some likely nineteenth century antiquarian editions. I had spent many an hour at flea markets and antiques shows picking through tables of battered old books and had rescued dozens of nineteenth century survivors myself. It intrigued me to know I was reading a classic book that was first opened a century or more before by someone who read it when it was newly-published and the author was still among the living.

Among Ellen's books I spotted one of my very favorite classics, Thomas Hardy's *Tess of the d'Urbervilles*, first published in 1891 in England. The full title of the book, *Tess of the d'Urbervilles: A Pure Woman Faithfully Represented*, sounds like some bio of a saint-like woman, an example to others of her sex. Not a chance. Tess, a farmer's daughter, wends her way through a life of victimization and abandonment leading to few choices, none of them good. Hardy questioned Christian morality and Victorian mores and used sex, violence, hypocrisy, and character cowardice to make his points, provoking mixed reviews and a good amount of controversy. Like Nathaniel Hawthorne in *The Scarlet Letter*,

Hardy excelled in his sensitive, insightful depiction of his young female protagonist. The layered, multifaceted creations that are Hawthorne's Hester Prynne and Hardy's Tess d'Urberville still resonate with readers and remain relevant in the context of the issues that face women to this day.

My copy of *Tess of the d'Urbervilles* is an early American edition printed in 1892, just a year after the first edition was released in England. Like the book title, the rusty-red front cover of the book, decorated with tiny shamrocks surrounding a gilt coat of arms, gives no indication of the stark realities of the story to come or the complexity of the themes in its pages. I could see from the spine of Ellen's copy that it had the same binding as mine and was no doubt a similarly early edition. I told Ellen how much I loved Hardy's book and how I loved *The Scarlet Letter* for similar reasons. She smiled and expressed her agreement and I promised myself I would sit down with her for a discussion about our mutual friend Tess before I left Sunrise for home.

Part Three:

Nicola

11. Who Do You Think You Are?

Among the things I took care of for Cat while she was at Sunrise was picking up her mail, tossing the junk mail, and bringing her the rest. I had brought over her checkbook so she could pay her bills and, if not paid on-line, I mailed them out at the post office. After the junk mail was disposed of, there wasn't a lot of mail remaining to be perused and dealt with. A few packages arrived with items ordered just before Cat wound up on the icy pavement, including a new pair of black patent leather pumps with narrow three-inch heels. It was an easy decision that those sexy kicks would be going back pronto as they were definitely not knee-friendly. There was one small package that came just after Cat went to Sunrise. It had me stumped. I took the box to Cat.

"Oh my God," she said. "I completely forgot about ordering this. Thanks for bring it over. Are you sure I didn't hit my head when I fell?"

"Did you forget that you have a tendency to be forgetful?" I said. "What is it?"

"It's a DNA test kit," she said as she broke the plastic seal and opened the box. "I'm going to find out about my ancient origins and how much Neanderthal I have in me."

"Nifty, but when did you get interested in genealogy and why?" I asked.

She hesitated before answering. I could see the wheels turning as she was deciding if she would give me a flip quip or the real answer to my question. She decided to come clean.

"It was a combination of things. Just before Gemma died, she had told me she wanted to take a genetics course as a science elective while she was in college. She thought that DNA research was 'cool.' After Nora died I suddenly realized that, biologically speaking, I was alone, no family left. I know I don't have to explain what I mean to you. Remember when I needed an emergency contact for the hospital after I fell? It's a bitch being a family of one."

That explanation was plausible enough when I heard it but much later I would find out that it was incomplete, the most important part having been omitted by Cat. Sometimes being 'alone' and a 'family of one' can translate to being an island surrounded by a moat or a fort encircled by a defensive wall, a secure place . . . something I do understand.

Cat offered me the option to step out while she spit (repeatedly) into the plastic vial that would be sent back to the DNA company for analysis. The enclosed rules had to be followed scrupulously, including the fact that saliva bubbles did not count in filling the vial up to the marked line. Cat went at it with gusto and soon the deed was done. She snapped the vial closed releasing a chemical agent that mixed with her saliva and prepared it for transport back to the DNA lab. Cat sealed up the return envelope and I dropped it off at the post office. It would be six or more weeks until the analysis was completed and Cat got the results.

I was often with Cat at Sunrise during the many months of Nora's devastating descent to death. I gave Cat all the support I could muster, even though she didn't make it easy. She is one of those people with a fierce sense of justice and a keenly empathetic nature, both of those traits fueling her desire to help others. She also has an equally fierce streak of independence and, when it came to accepting help or support, she was clueless and instinctively resistant. I resorted to telling her that even if she felt she didn't need my support, Nora would have it. She couldn't argue with that.

Cat shared very little of her thoughts and feelings about Nora's daily struggles in the memory care unit. I never saw a tear but I know she must have shed many for the woman who was her surrogate mother and also her friend. Losing Nora, as she told me when talking about the DNA testing, meant a transition to yet another level of aloneness. I once read an article in the *Wall Street Journal* about so-called 'adult orphans,' people facing a future without either of their parents for the first time and struggling with the void created by their loss, particularly during the holidays. I got that. So did Cat.

She mourned Nora's passing with her typical emotional restraint. She honored Nora's wishes for her wake and burial, dealt with clearing out Nora's room at Sunrise and efficiently donated items to local charities. Nora was laid to rest with Cat's mother Moira, next to Gemma and Rick's graves.

Even when we indulged in a bit too much wine, a time when I was prone to being more inclined to confessions and sharing, Cat did not lower the bridge over her moat and let me in. To be truthful, both of us were still holding back, each in our own way and for our own reasons. No piece of paper making us each other's emergency contact or healthcare proxy made us truly *family* and we had yet to realize that not all definitions of family involve biology, especially in today's world. Beyond that, there were the risks that came with opening yourself up completely to someone, among them the chance that those revelations would change how they felt about you or fracture a friendship. As they say: proceed with caution.

12. The Elder Orphans Club

Cat had a birthday during her weeks at Sunrise – a decade-ender that some women (and men) describe as a horror show double feature: seeing your (prior) life flash before your eyes, immediately followed by a mental slideshow of soon-to-arrive official senior citizenship. Yep, the age-old question 'where the hell did the time go' was about to be replaced by 'wonder how much time is left.'

I had stepped off that dreaded birthday cliff a few years earlier without much angst or fanfare. A couple years after that when I was eligible to collect early Social Security benefits, I demurred telling myself I didn't need the money. Truth be told I just wasn't ready to queue up at the Social Security office and get on the dole that marked me as officially *old*. In a matter of months I will have to hold my nose and jump in to register for Medicare. Guess I'll kill two birds with one stone and sign up for the check at the same time.

Cat's temporary housemates at Sunrise, who enjoyed any occasion for indulging in a celebration and the treats that came with it, dove into the sparkling cider and birthday cupcakes I brought over. I had made sixty of them, each numbered in consecutive order, along with another dozen, each of those decorated with an exclamation point for emphasis. There was good-natured joking about Cat joining them as a newly-minted senior citizen and a number of offers of the loan of a cane or walker should she need one. She loved every minute of it, corny jokes and sincere warm wishes alike. It was good to see her smile in a place that once brought her only sadness and heartache.

I don't mean to paint a picture of Sunrise as some kind of resort for the elderly. No amount of wine in plastic cups, birthday celebrations, or minibus rides to Walmart could change the fact that Sunrise was an end-of-life station stop. My own grandmother had passed the last months of her life in a nursing home when I was about ten years old and I have vivid recollections of going there with my mother. That nursing home was decent but nothing near the accommodations, atmosphere, and array of activities offered at Sunrise. When we visited my grandmother and walked down the main corridor to her room, we were greeted by invalid residents in wheelchairs lined up all along the way. As we passed them, many would reach out to us, trying to get us to stop. They were particularly drawn to young children but would also often ask my mother if she was their daughter. My mother would stop and gently tell them that she wasn't rather than ignoring them and walking on. Mother explained to me that many of them never got any visitors and we should be kind and gentle with them. I adored my grandmother and was very glad that we visited her so often, even when she didn't seem to know we were there. I once heard my mother tell my aunt (who also visited regularly) that my grandmother would get better care due to our frequent visits as the staff would know we were watching out for her. I remember seeing my mother occasionally slip a staff member a five dollar bill to keep an extra eye on my grandmother. I was gutted when I lost my grandmother but, even at my young age, I felt relief that she was no longer in that nursing home.

In the weeks that Cat was convalescing at Sunrise, I got to know many of the residents and couldn't help noticing the ones who got visitors and those who did not. For those in the assisted living wing, friendships with other residents often filled the void resulting from a lack of contact with people in the outside world. In the memory care unit, most of the residents were no longer capable of engaging with visitors or with those living with them. All these years after my grandmother's death, I still can't shake the feeling that even if a resident is unable to interact with them, visitors represent a form of patient advocacy, albeit a subtle or subliminal one.

While I was pondering the past and present states of institutional care and making my observations about life at Sunrise, I happened upon an internet piece on the topic of *elder orphans*, a seeming tangent of the adult orphan article I had previously read. So, if an adult orphan was a non-elderly person who had lost both parents to death, what the hell was an elder orphan? The piece basically described elder orphans as seniors who are single or widowed with no children (at least none living locally and available to them) and no other support system. So, at a time when they are most vulnerable, they find themselves alone with no one to help care for them directly or to oversee their institutional care. This already sad terminology was made more troubling by a prediction of the expected significant increase in elder orphans due to the graying of the baby boomer generation. God save us from the continuing onslaught of gloom and doom aimed at our boomer generation . . . and from our fellow boomers who, at the other end of the spectrum, keep chanting that sixty is the new forty!

Being a temporary resident at Sunrise, Cat had even more opportunity to know many of the regulars and we sometimes shared our observations about them. I once heard the facility director comment that sometimes her role was akin to being a high school counselor or disciplinarian dealing with a bunch of adolescents, settling disputes, and soothing wounded feelings. She didn't say it in a derogatory way. Communal living in general comes with challenges. Adding the onslaught of mental and physical fragilities in the elderly ratchets that up a notch or two. Cat spent the most time with Ellen McNally, their mutual connection with Cat's Aunt Nora being the initial basis for their new friendship but there was more to it. They discovered a common interest in reading classic literature and enjoyed discussing their favorite stories and characters.

One evening as they sat together in Ellen's rooms, Cat mentioned the DNA test results she was awaiting and Ellen proved very curious about how the test was taken and what kind of results it might provide. Not long after, another small white box arrived at Cat's house and I recognized the packaging. It was another DNA test kit. I brought the box over to Cat and she confirmed that it was for Ellen but offered no further explanation. The spitting was done and Cat asked me to mail the kit back for her. I really wanted to ask why a 79-year-old woman without husband, children, or other living family was embarking on a genealogical search and what exactly she hoped to discover . . . but I didn't. I hoped Cat would clue me in and trusted that, if she didn't, it was because she had promised Ellen her privacy.

13. *Sometimes I Feel Like a Motherless Child*

Cat made continued progress with her rehab and took full advantage of the weeks of therapy that her insurance plan provided. She left Sunrise in pretty good shape and continued outpatient physical therapy as prescribed by her orthopedist for the next two months, determined to do everything possible to rebuild her atrophied thigh muscles and maximize the recovery and future use of her knee.

She had progressed from an enormous leg brace to a less obtrusive knee brace and had learned to use crutches when she was not allowed to put weight on the injured leg. She had slept for weeks in those braces and, a side-sleeper, had to learn to sleep on her back. I remember the day she was once again allowed to take a shower. She was petrified to stand in the tub alone but soldiered through it . . . with me sitting nearby on the toilet, just in case. These were just some of the ordeals she went through for months as she slowly regained her strength, knee flexibility, and so her independence. I saw how much she had to deal with and how she did all of it without complaining or feeling sorry for herself. She channeled her innate determination and problem-solving mindset and just pushed forward. The culmination was the day, three months after she fell, when the doctor gave her the ok to drive.

Cat's DNA test results arrived a few weeks after she returned home from Sunrise. I was still wondering if I really knew why Cat suddenly decided to take the test but, if there was more to it than she had told me, I would just have to wait for her to share. I was at Cat's house when the envelope arrived. She tore it open and scanned the enclosed official summary results certificate. The full report had to be accessed on-line where ethnic percentages with explanatory information were broken down and a 'frequently asked questions' function was available. A few days after that envelope arrived, I bit the bullet and asked Cat about the results, knowing there was no way she had not gone on-line to comb through the full report.

"Well Nic, I'm 98% European and just about all of that points to the fair Emerald Isle," she said. "The rest is composed of wisps of North Africa, the Middle East/Caucasus, and Iberian peninsula. It's all but a road map of the journey of early humankind out of Africa, into the Middle East, west to Spain and then up to Britain and

Ireland in small boats. No traces of Scandinavia so at least I'm not one of those Irish descended from marauding bands of Viking invaders."

"So, no surprises," I said. "You never told me anything about your father Cat. He must have been Irish or Irish-American like your mother then?"

With that shot across the bow delivered, I closed my mouth not sure if Cat would shut me down or tell me about the father she had never spoken about in the decade I had known her. She exhaled audibly, closed her eyes, and downed the last swallows of wine in her glass. After refilling her wine glass and mine, she answered my question with several of her own.

"My father? Which one?" she said. "Do you mean the ne'er-do-well father who Moira and Nora never wanted to talk about because, as it turns out, he didn't exist? Or, do you mean the man who actually fathered me?"

"I don't understand," I said.

"Well, that makes two of us. Oh, I should mention that my mother Moira wasn't actually my mother, biologically speaking anyway. For nearly sixty years, first Moira and then Nora lied to me about who I was . . . who I am."

"Jesus Christ Cat, please tell me what the hell is going on and start at the beginning," I said.

For the next half hour, Cat slowly told me how she found out that everything she believed about her family was predicated on a web of lies and organized deceit. When her Aunt Nora died Cat, a 'fallen away' Catholic, did what she knew Nora would have wanted. She contacted Nora's parish priest, Father Aloysius at St. Columba's, and arranged for a proper Catholic funeral mass and burial in the church cemetery. Nora's will included a memorial bequest to St. Columba's and, a week after the funeral, when Cat answered the front door bell to find Father Aloysius, she wondered if he was there to collect. He was not. He had instead come to carry out another of Nora's requests.

Cat ushered him in and offered him a cup of coffee, which he accepted. As they sat across from each other at the small kitchen table, he appeared uncomfortable. After taking a sip of his coffee, he pulled an envelope from his inside jacket pocket. He told Cat it contained a letter to her from Nora, a letter that Nora had asked him to read before sealing the envelope about two years earlier. He was to hold the letter until Nora's death and then give it to Cat. He handed the envelope to Cat but she did not immediately open it as he might have expected. Instead, she simply (and probably a bit curtly) asked him if he would like to tell her what was in it since he had known about it for two years. He got the message, demurred and rose from the chair saying that, should she want to, he would be available to talk with her after she read the letter. With that, he headed to the front door and made his escape.

Cat sensed that the letter brought no good news. What could Nora have had to say to her that she couldn't just tell her while she was alive? The fact that she felt compelled to tell the priest the secret smacked of Catholic guilt and some type of confession scenario. The unopened envelope lay on the kitchen table for three days during which time Cat gave it the evil eye on a regular basis. Listening to her, I thought of the time I had a cardiac test and waited anxiously for the results. After a week of angst and no call from the doctor, my frustration and fear spilled over and I took myself over to the radiology center and asked for a copy of the results. I took that sealed envelope, brought it home and then lost my nerve. When I did open it, I did so just the way we learned to take off an old bandage when we were kids; I yanked it open and happily read that everything was ok.

When Cat opened Nora's letter, her suspicions were more than justified. It was a hell of a confession all right. The gist was that Moira was not Cat's mother (and Nora, in kind, was not her aunt). There was no ne'er-do-well absentee father who had deserted them. Cat was adopted.

There was more. One evening while Cat was staying at Sunrise, she stopped by Ellen's rooms for a visit and the expected proffered cup of Taylors of Harrogate tea. Cat had had a tough day of rehab but despite being tired she had sought Ellen out. Since she had arrived at Sunrise to find Nora's friend Ellen still there, she had toyed with the idea that Nora might have confided in Ellen, perhaps telling her something about Cat's adoption. She decided it was time to ask.

With a cup of Assam steeping in front of her, Cat blurted out her question. "Ellen, did Nora ever tell you that I was not her biological niece . . . or Moira's biological daughter?"

Ellen slowly lowered her cup back to its saucer. Her eyes met Cat's as she responded. "Never," was her answer. "Why would you think that?"

Cat followed up with another question. "Why would I think that Nora confided that to you or why would I think I was adopted?"

"Both," Ellen said, "but most importantly, why do you think that you were adopted?"

As her tea got cold, Cat told Ellen about the visit from Father Aloysius and the confessional letter from Nora. Cat has a gift for reading people. As she explains it, she is an 'intuiter' and just 'sees things' when dealing with people, as if looking through a veil that gives her a peek at what is behind the things people say and do. Her 'Spidey sense' told her Nora had not told Ellen anything about Cat's adoption.

Ellen asked Cat the same thing I asked: What was she going to do now that she knew the truth? I suspect that Ellen already knew Cat well enough to know the answer. I had. Cat would move heaven and earth to find out who she was, overturning every rock, shaking every tree, pursuing every lead until she discovered the truth. After some months of struggling with feelings of betrayal, Cat had come to grips with her new 'reality.' The journey to unlock her true origins and identity had begun with her decision to do the DNA test.

Part Four:

Caitriona & Ellen

14. Trading Places

I don't know why I waited so long to tell Nic. It would have been better for me had I told her much sooner. Sharing a secret... or a heartache... puts another set of shoulders under its yoke and can't help but make the burden lighter for the one that does the sharing. Feelings of anger and betrayal had burned in my gut for weeks, months really.

Nora's letter was a short and sweet confessional that included no details about my biological origins. With Nora safely resting in her grave, there was no opportunity for me to ask her the questions that swirled in my mind. More than that, I was robbed of the chance to confront her about her deceit. Nora's escape left me in a situation over which I felt I had no control. I don't do *no control*. I don't let the waves of life buffet me to and fro and I don't like surprises. Intuiters really don't like surprises. Surprises are an affront to our gift of seeing behind the veils in our daily lives.

I finally invited Nic to join me under the yoke of my secret after Ellen McNally shared her own secret with me, that revelation necessitating that I shift one of my shoulders under Ellen's yoke. It was time to call in reinforcements to help bear the weight of these burdens. After her initial shock as reflected in a look of confusion accompanied by a taking of the Lord's name in vain, Nic was at the ready in any way I wanted or needed and I felt the weight shift off me immediately. I had one more dilemma, however. In coming clean with Nic about being adopted, I still had to keep Ellen's confidence and not tell Nic about Ellen's secret. Keeping the orbits of secrets among friends from intersecting is a tricky thing. One slip of the tongue and the jig is up. So, while sharing a secret (with the right person) can bring relief to the one doing the sharing, being a faithful steward of what is shared with you can be a risky business.

When I had suddenly and bluntly asked Ellen if Nora had told her I was adopted, I had unintentionally forced opened Ellen's own private Pandora's box. Her personal demons overcame her after decades of being bound by her determined silence. In the original Greek mythological tale, Pandora actually opens a jar that contains all the evils in the world. When she is able to recap the jar, all that remains is the spirit of hope. It took a while but, ultimately, Ellen's confession would restore *her* hope.

My instincts told me that Nora had not told Ellen I was adopted. Still, when I asked her the question, a blanched look of trepidation came over her face. While it might have been sympathy for my situation, I was sure it wasn't. I recognized it as empathy, not sympathy, and I sensed she was struggling under the weight of it. What I didn't know was the effect that an unexpected confrontation with an adoptee in search of her mother would have on Ellen. When I had pulled back the bow string and released my arrow of inquiry in Ellen's direction, I had hit the very heart of my target. From that wound poured forth an unbelievable tale of love and loss that had lived deep in the recesses of Ellen's heart and mind for some six decades.

Ellen was born and raised in Callaway, West Virginia. She has almost no recollections of her father as he died in a work accident in 1940 when she was almost five years old. Ellen's life with her widowed mother was a hardscrabble day-to-day existence. Rural poverty meant doing without and barely keeping a ramshackle roof over their heads. During the harvest season, Ellen joined her mother at local orchards where she picked apples alongside migrant workers. One of the farm foremen, a tall, muscular man named Ernie, would sometimes give Ellen an apple to eat while her mother was picking. In time, Ernie and Ellen's mother Sara married and, at first, it seemed their small family would be a happy one.

Ernie had been in the Marines during World War II and, as Ellen and her mother soon discovered, he was plagued by dreams and flashbacks of the terrible things he had seen and experienced while fighting in the Pacific. Sometimes, to escape those awful dreams and painful memories, he resorted to drinking and the alcohol he hoped would soothe him instead made him mean. In his drunken rantings, Ernie would sometimes lash out at Sara, blaming her for not getting pregnant and giving him a child, something he clearly expected out of their marriage. Sara would try to reason with him (to no avail), telling him she too hoped that, in time, they would have a child together.

When Ellen was sixteen, her mother Sara began to have stomach problems. Plagued by nausea and vomiting, Sara and Ernie thought that, finally, Sara was pregnant. Ernie was ecstatic. He curtailed his daily drinking and doted on Sara. As the weeks went by, the nausea and vomiting continued and, one morning, Sara went to the bathroom and returned ashen-faced, pointing to her groin and telling Ernie that she was bleeding. Ernie immediately feared a miscarriage and rushed her to the local doctor. In the end they would find out that it was not a miscarriage as there had not been any pregnancy. Sara had cancer and the prognosis was dire. Ellen gave her dying mother tender and loving care during the few months leading up to Sara's death. Ernie withdrew from both of them and turned to the bottle once again for his consolation.

After Sara's death, Ellen attempted to reach out to Ernie to no effect. She remained patient and took the lead in keeping the household running while attending school. She preferred Ernie being distant and uncommunicative (as he often was) to his mean moods when drunk. When harvest time came once again, she took work picking apples as she had done for so many years with her mother. Picking gave her the solitude she craved and a feeling of once again being close to her mother. The extra money was a help as well. Ellen soon decided that when she graduated the following June, she would leave home and make a new start . . . somewhere. With that in mind, she put aside some of the money she was earning apple picking. She wasn't sure where she would go or what Ernie's reaction would be but her mind was made up to go.

As we all know, the best laid plans can often be upset by people and things we could not have imagined or anticipated. So it was with Ellen's plan to escape West Virginia, high school diploma in hand and a small getaway fund in her wallet.

15. Mary Ellen Stuart

As I listened to Ellen go on with her story, I wondered if it would have been better for her to make her confessions to Father Aloysius instead of to me. I didn't know if Ellen was a practicing Catholic or if she embraced any religious faction or faith but, in short order, I knew this was going to be a world-class conscience purge. Who was going to give Ellen the penance and absolution equal to that purging? Isn't that the point of confessing . . . to be cleansed and forgiven?

Ellen's tale continued with the revelation that she was born Mary Ellen Stuart, *Mary* for her paternal grandmother and *Ellen* for her mother Sara's mother. Jumping right in and knowing that Ellen had never married, I asked why she changed her name and where the name McNally came from.

Ellen sighed. "McNally was my grandmother Ellen's maiden name. Why I became Ellen McNally is a question that will take a lot longer to answer."

During the years that Ellen picked apples with her mother, it was common for them to work alongside migrant workers who came to the area for the picking season and then moved on. While Ellen's mother Sara was not overly friendly to the migrants, she was a tolerant person and schooled Ellen not to imitate the prejudices of some of the locals who resented and looked down on the migrants. After Sara's death, when Ellen returned to apple picking on her own for the first time, the sight of the migrants working in the orchards with her brought her mother's words back to her. One afternoon, bending over and struggling to move a basket laden with newly-picked apples, she saw another pair of hands suddenly gripping the rim of the basket.

"Let me help you," said a young male voice.

Ellen turned toward the voice and looked up into a pair of large dark brown eyes. Getting nowhere with moving the basket on her own, she accepted the offered help. That fateful encounter set off a chain of events that gave birth to 'Ellen McNally.'

The young man who came to Ellen's aid in the orchard was Mateo Soto, the eldest son of a migrant family that had come from the Southwest for the picking season in West Virginia. Muscular, with olive skin and jet black hair set off by a brilliant white smile, he was the most striking young man Ellen had ever seen. For Mateo, Ellen's pale porcelain skin, blue eyes, and blonde hair made just as striking an impression.

First by chance, and then with planning, Ellen and Mateo managed to see each other in the orchards and, later, they met secretly elsewhere. Ellen, who had been so closed up emotionally for so long, was overcome with a rush of feelings she had never before experienced. Her world of solitude crumbled, replaced by a world that centered on Mateo. His words soothed her, his talk about the future made her optimistic once again, his caresses bound her to him emotionally to the depths of her soul.

Mateo was, in his turn, just as devoted to Ellen. He longed for her whenever they were apart and treasured every moment he spent with her. His life must be with her, their futures would be one.

The young lovers were very aware that the picking season would end meaning separation for them. Mateo told Ellen he would speak to his parents and ask them to allow Ellen to travel with them, leaving West Virginia and Ellen's stepfather Ernie behind. She could join the Soto family and eventually marry Mateo when the time was right.

Ellen had met Mr. and Mrs. Soto who, after some initial awkwardness, were very kind and welcoming to her. Still, she knew that asking them to do what Mateo wanted was something risky, even dangerous for them. She was nearing her 18th birthday, as was Mateo, and expected that Ernie would not try to track her down when she was so close to being legally an adult. Still, for migrants, very likely illegal immigrants, interfering with a white family could bring terrible consequences.

Ellen would never know if Mr. and Mrs. Soto would have agreed to help her leave West Virginia with them. Just minutes after Mateo had told her he planned to ask them, their rendezvous in an old shed near the orchards ended violently when Ernie stormed in on them. He was drunk . . . mean drunk.

"You filthy little whore," he bellowed as he grabbed Ellen's arm and yanked her up off the ground. He slapped her so hard her head snapped back, blood trickled from her nose and she went limp.

Mateo jumped up and swung wildly at Ernie, trying to free Ellen from his grasp. Still dazed, Ellen threw up her free arm to shield Mateo from a blow with a rusty old rake wielded by Ernie. Her arm deflected some of the force of the rake but the teeth hit Mateo squarely in the face, striking his forehead, cutting a nasty gash across his cheek and sending him down to the ground seemingly unconscious.

Ernie literally dragged Ellen all the way home, slapping her again every time she resisted and attempted to get free to go back to Mateo. When he got her into the house, he threw her on the rug near the hearth and continued to call her a whore and a slut. He took up the bottle and drank as he screamed, getting more angry with each gulp of alcohol. Standing over her, one of his legs on each side of her hips, he suddenly grew quiet.

"I'll show you what a real man can do with a little whore like you," he growled.

In seconds he was on top of her tearing at her clothes and unzipping his pants. He stunk of booze and sweat and his drool fell on her face and neck. Ellen scratched at him and tried to get loose only to be slapped and pawed all the more. Somehow, in her panic and white-hot fear, her hand brushed against a small log lying next to the hearth. Suddenly Ernie slumped on top of her. She squirmed free, rolling him off her and only then realized she had the small log in her hand.

Survival instinct still in control, she grabbed her few clothes, the small stash of money she was saving and a framed photo of her mother and ran from the house. She went to the old shed praying she wouldn't find Mateo dead there. She opened the creaking wood door and found no one.

In that moment, facing a life-changing crossroads, she decided she must flee on her own and never come back. If she went to Mateo and his parents, they would be implicated in what happened to Ernie. As migrants, they would likely be dealt with harshly and unfairly and, if she had killed Ernie, they might be charged with murder. She loved Mateo too much to expose him to that risk. Ignorance and distance from her would be his best protections.

16. Ellen McNally

At the moment when Ellen stepped up onto the Greyhound bus destined for New York City, frightened fugitive Mary Ellen Stuart ceased to exist. All traces of Mary Ellen were to be snuffed out, never again to be spoken of or acknowledged in any other way . . . and they were . . . for more than a half-century. Mary Ellen's former space was instantly filled by Ellen McNally, an aspiring young woman pursuing a completely new life. Ellen likened it to a shedding snake that literally slithers out of and abandons its skin, never looking back at its former shell.

The first thing Ellen discovered about her new persona was that she didn't travel well on public transportation. About an hour into the trip, Ellen's stomach began to roil and she struggled to keep down the bile that was rising to her throat. Head in her hands, she tried to fend off her increasing nausea. What could she throw up she wondered? She hadn't eaten a meal since the afternoon before and had only snacked on a candy bar since.

A middle-aged woman across the aisle leaned over and extended her hand, offering a small brown paper bag, whispering that she often got 'bus-sick' herself and came prepared, just in case. Just the sight of the paper bag was enough to trigger Ellen to heave and she barely got the bag to her mouth in time. The kind woman across the aisle provided tissues and then a stick of peppermint gum. She wasn't kidding about being prepared.

With her stomach achingly empty and a feeling of exhaustion overtaking her, Ellen slept fitfully for most of the rest of the trip. She started awake, momentarily unsure of where she was, in response to an announcement of arrival at the Greyhound terminal adjacent to Pennsylvania Station. Both terminal and station were hives of activity, the competing sounds of rushing (sometimes running) feet, blaring public announcement systems, and the engine noise of trains and buses assaulting the ears. Ellen scanned the bustling expanse around her, polished stone floors to vaulted ceilings, her neck craning, eyes wide, and mouth agape. She suspected there were more people around her in those moments than the total number of people living in Callaway and its outskirts. Suddenly, she felt a rush of heat and the urge to vomit returned with a vengeance.

She made it to the bathroom stall just in time for a short but intense episode of cramping and retching that tossed the last bits of stomach contents up and out. Looking at herself in the cracked mirror over one of the bathroom sinks she saw her whitewashed pallor and a broken blood vessel in her one eye, no doubt the result of the strain of her heaving. She washed her hands and then soaked a paper towel in cool tap water, wrung it out a bit, and wiped her face and neck. When she looked into the mirror once again, she saw a woman watching her. The woman was young, early thirties perhaps, with dark brown hair combed straight back and secured at the nape of her neck. She wore a plain button down white shirt under a navy blue jumper, an austere look for a person of her age. Ellen saw the woman smiling at her in the mirror glass and turned toward her noticing a wooden crucifix worn around her neck on a thin braided cord.

"Are you all right dear?" said the woman. "Do you need help or medical attention?"

Ellen explained that she had just arrived, had found her long bus ride hard on her stomach and was hoping the worst was over at that point. As they exited the rest room, the woman asked Ellen if she was going to a friend or relative or needed to make arrangements for a place to stay that night. When Ellen hesitated in answering, the woman explained she was part of a group affiliated with a local Catholic parish and was there with another group member for the specific purpose of providing assistance to newly-arrived young girls who were alone and in need of help in finding a safe, inexpensive place to stay.

Perhaps if Ellen had been more street-smart, she would have been suspicious of the woman's motives but, with her rural upbringing, she took the woman at her word. In fact the woman, whose name was Margot Addison, was exactly what she said she was. The tradition of church-affiliated volunteers looking out for young girls and women newly-arrived in the 'big city' unescorted and without local connections goes back at least to the mid-19th century and the waves of female immigrants coming to America seeking a new, more prosperous life. One of the groups doing that in New York City in the second half of the 1800s was the Mission of Our Lady of the Rosary for the Protection of Irish Immigrant Girls. Over the decades of its existence, the Mission provided a temporary home to tens of thousands of young girls who arrived in New York by ship and found themselves alone on the docks and without the connections or ability to safely proceed on their journey. Ellen's own personal missionary, Margot Addison, became both her counselor and a friend, directing Ellen to a respectable, economical rooming house for single women and also helping her find her first job at a Horn & Hardart automat in Manhattan.

Talking about those days and her responsibilities at the automat brought a soft smile to Ellen's face for the first time since she began to tell me her secret story. For a few minutes she reminisced about her time at Horn & Hardart, describing her crisp black uniform and the very structured procedures that governed the operation of the automat. Her first job was out of the public eye. She was one of the many unseen workers behind the serving machines who hustled to refill the contents of empty compartments. Others kept the buffet-style steaming tables full of piping hot food choices.

After a few weeks, she was also trained to work out on the floor of the huge dining hall as a cashier. Sitting up straight-backed in a glass booth and equipped with rubber fingertip covers, she greeted diners and exchanged their paper currency, dimes, and quarters for the nickels needed for the vending machines.

"I was what they called a 'nickel thrower' and a very quick and capable one," she said impishly. "The aroma of hot coffee, fresh pie and other delicious food, displayed and served in sparkling clean surroundings . . . it was something. Our uniforms were black for a practical reason – as we handled money hour after hour, our hands were soon as black as our clothing!"

Ellen continued on listing out dozens of the hundreds of menu items and describing the eclectic mix of clientele that included famous actors and writers, business people . . . and the poor and struggling who could only afford to buy a small portion but lingered at their table taking in the sights and savoring their food.

Watching Ellen's face, I almost thought I saw a glimpse of the 17-year-old country girl she once was and I imagined her stomach aflutter on the first day she put on her well-starched uniform and reported to work. I was born in the mid-1950s in New York around the time Ellen sought refuge there. Too young to have my own memories of that post-war decade, Ellen's story had me recalling old black-and-white photos of me with Nora and Moira taken when I was a toddler. I remembered their perfectly ironed dresses with fitted bodices that emphasized their small waists and then flared out in full feminine skirts that flattered their legs. No outfit was complete without gloves and a hat that coordinated perfectly and, oh, those shoes!

17. God Bless the Child

Ellen had poured forth her story with all the energy and urgency that had built up over decades of forcibly containing it. I wanted to interrupt her to ask questions but the tale came in fierce waves that could not be held back or diverted . . . and, as it turns out, the story was far from its end. I had no choice but to wait and let my list of questions grow, item number one being whether Ellen had killed her stepfather Ernie when she struck him with the log.

When Ellen had finished reminiscing about her time working at the automat, the warm smile faded from her face as she took a deep breath before continuing. I could see that the clouds were returning and I knew what was coming could not be anything good.

"Remember the vomiting on the bus and in the terminal?" she asked. "Well, I wasn't bus-sick. I was pregnant."

Those two sentences were delivered with naked directness as she lifted her chin and looked me straight in the eye. She paused to let it sink in, giving me the opening to ask one of the many questions I had been waiting to ask but, a bit stunned and at a loss for words, I said nothing. That moment passed in deadly silence and Ellen quickly dove back in, continuing the story and saving me from an awkward situation.

Ellen explained that she had been intimate with Mateo only once when their passion had overtaken them. She said she had never felt so close to another person in her life and described the experience as being made whole for the first time, utterly bound physically and emotionally to Mateo. She said that the look of awe on Mateo's flushed face told her everything she needed to know about how he was feeling. It never occurred to Ellen that she might get pregnant from that one encounter.

It was Margot Addison who suspected that Ellen might be pregnant. Ellen protested that it could not be possible but eventually admitted that she and her boyfriend had sex once. Once was enough. Ellen was going to have a baby. Margot's charitable work extended to activities supporting a Catholic unwed mothers home operated under the auspices of an order of nuns. Despite her good fortune of having Margot looking out for her, Ellen alternated between near-panic attacks and periods of mild depression. One of her co-workers at Horn and Hardart told her about a 'doctor' who helped girls like Ellen end their pregnancies . . . for a steep price.

In response to that suggestion, Ellen had reflexively placed her two hands protectively on her belly and, at that moment, she knew for the first time she wanted her baby.

Ellen worked as long as she was able, saving every penny she could in anticipation of the baby's birth. When Ellen's pregnancy became obvious, her supervisor Mr. Turner asked her to step into his office. She was sure he would fire her knowing she was pregnant and not married. Before that could happen, she took the bull by the horns and thanked him for letting her continue to work during her pregnancy and, forcing some tears, explained that she was a widow, having lost her husband in a mining accident and then discovering she was expecting his child. Turner, already uncomfortable at the thought of having to terminate an unwed mother, was unprepared for Ellen's preemptive strike. Left with the choice of calling her a liar or going along with her story, he chose to accept it. As Ellen closed Mr. Turner's door behind her, she flushed red with shame at how easily she had concocted the story of being a widow.

Aside from some nasty morning sickness in her first trimester, Ellen's pregnancy went smoothly. "Yes," she told me, "in my case, the 'p' in the word pregnancy stood for puking."

Ellen began living at the unwed mothers home, St. Gerard's, about six weeks before her due date. After only two weeks there, her water suddenly broke and she doubled over in pain. Before she knew it she was in the delivery room, scared to death as she lay on a gurney. That was the last thing she remembered until the tones of Margot Addison's voice brought her back to consciousness.

"Ellen," she said softly, "your baby is here . . . actually . . . both of your babies are here. You had twin girls."

Beyond that, Ellen's recollections of the time immediately after she gave birth are foggy. Sometime later when she felt stronger and the medication haze had receded, she asked to see her daughters. When the door opened, rather than the babies being brought in, Margot came in and pulled up a chair next to the bed.

"Ellen," said Margot, "there is something I must tell you." Without preamble she went right to the point. "One of the babies is healthy and doing well. The other baby has problems, serious problems. She is Mongoloid and has other serious medical issues."

"That's what they called Down syndrome in those days," Ellen said drily. "My babies were fraternal twins; they didn't look alike. One was *perfect* they told me. I guess that made the other one *defective* – at least that's how they unintentionally made me feel. To me, they were both beautiful. Still, when I thought of taking care of two babies, one of them needing so much, I began to have anxiety attacks. My heart would pound as if it would fly out of my chest and my breathing came in short, shallow gulps. After days of those episodes, Margot sat me down with an adoption counselor to discuss my 'options.' I didn't need a counselor, I had already made my decision. I would give my 'perfect' daughter up for adoption so she would have the best possible chance at a better life than I could give her. I would give myself to her sister, who I named Tamsin, meaning 'twin.' I would be the best mother I could be for my little broken angel for as long as I had her."

Ellen paused and reached for the delicate silver chain that hung around her neck. She pulled it upward, revealing a small pendant. She lowered her head as she fingered it, slowly rubbing the pendant between her thumb and forefinger as if to soothe herself. I saw a single tear travel down her lined cheek.

"I was so distraught about giving my daughter up for adoption that I almost reneged. I didn't know how I would live without her, with the knowledge that I gave her away, and without knowing what became of her. The nuns told me a wonderful home had been found for my baby with a couple who had been unable to have children of their own. She would be loved, cherished, and raised in a comfortable Catholic home. They told me the baby would be picked up in two days but that was a lie. The baby was taken to the adoptive parents at the same time I was in the Mother Superior's office being told it would happen in two days. I raged when I found out how they tricked me and I thought they would kick me out . . . but they didn't. They wisely gave me some space and brought Tamsin to me for a feeding. As I looked into her eyes, the same color blue as my own, I calmed and focused on how Tamsin and I would live."

As I listened to Ellen, I had waves of competing thoughts and emotions. She had given away her baby, just as my birth mother had given me away, in her case all but forced to make that terrible choice. Could my own mother have been in an equally untenable situation when she gave me up? Had I rushed to judgment when I found out I was adopted, blaming everyone from my birth mother to Moira and Nora without knowing the facts? Would I ever know the real story of my conception, birth, and adoption?

My surging thoughts were interrupted when Ellen, clearly spent, asked if I would come back the following day as she did not feel able to continue the story. Of course I said I would. Before leaving I suggested she undress and get ready for bed while I made her a cup of hot chocolate. I brought it to her bedside, sat with her while she sipped it and then took the cup to the sink, washed it out, and went back to my own room.

I slept very little that night, overtaken by my churning thoughts. I remembered the DNA test I had sent in and imagined finding my own birth mother once I had the results. My last stray thought before falling asleep was that there is a character called Tamsin in Thomas Hardy's book *The Return of the Native*, a story about people making choices that bring them heartache and loss. Hardy's take on the flaws and frailties of human nature, the power and promise of love, and the influence exerted on people by their communities and society at large remains timeless and perfectly applicable to our modern world.

18. For Every Bad

I sat with Ellen the following afternoon. After our usual cup of tea, Ellen resumed her story once again. There was no happy ending coming. A quote from Thomas Hardy would aptly sum up the remainder of Ellen's story: "For every bad, there is a worse."

Ellen's looming predicament about how she and the baby would live was unexpectedly solved when she and Tamsin were invited to stay on at St. Gerard's, at least for the near future. She would help with the running of the home, doing whatever tasks or chores were needed. Ellen later found out that unwed mothers of seriously ill or disabled babies were sometimes offered the sanctuary of staying on with the nuns, the thought being that their babies would likely not survive very long and the young mothers would need support during their ongoing tribulations.

Ellen gratefully accepted the offer to stay and strove to do everything she could in return. She did laundry, ironed, and cleaned at first. The Mother Superior, seeing how Ellen loved to read and observing that she helped the less literate expectant mothers write letters, asked Ellen to assist her with managing accounts and purchasing supplies. Ellen excelled at both and her organizational skills and detail orientation proved to be a great help in the running of St. Gerard's administrative operations.

While St. Gerard's was no doubt a safe haven for herself and Tamsin, it was somewhat like living in a bubble and sometimes Ellen longed to be independent and out in the world once again. She began making tentative plans to do just that, even thinking of asking if she might stay on as an employee after moving out to her own apartment. In that way she could bring Tamsin with her to work and would not need someone to care for her while she was working. It sounded so reasonable and doable in theory but, as the months went by, Tamsin's health was precarious and that situation took precedence over any plans or future hopes. Ellen's facial expressions told me as much as her words as she described Tamsin's deteriorating health.

"Oh Caitríona," murmured Ellen, "Tamsin was truly God's little angel, just lent to me as a special gift. She was so loving, the very soul of pure innocence. No matter how ill she was, she smiled the sweetest smile. When she would look up into my eyes and call me 'Mama,' my heart would swell with pure joy."

Tamsin fought her illnesses to the bitter end, rallying time and time again and defying the odds. She was her mother's daughter, resilient and unwilling to give up. Tamsin's fight ended just two months before her second birthday. Her death brought waves of grief to both Ellen and the nuns of St. Gerard's who loved Tamsin as a dear aunt or devoted grandmother would love a precious child.

More than once, as she talked, Ellen pulled out the pendant on the silver chain and unconsciously rubbed it between her fingers. After telling me about Tamsin's death, she pulled it out once more, deliberately, and extended it in my direction. I saw that the pendant was in the shape of half of a heart, a broken heart with a jagged border, and was engraved with just a date: 6-14-53. The engraving was faint, no doubt the result of years of Ellen's fingers rubbing back and forth across the numbers.

"Ellen," I said softly, "please tell me about the pendant."

"The pendant was a gift from one of the nuns at St. Gerard's," she said. "On the day Tamsin's sister was taken away and given to her adoptive parents, Sister Mary Cecilia came to my room and brought Tamsin to me, asking me to nurse her. I was still hot with anger over being deceived about when Tamsin's sister was to be handed over to her new parents. I glared at Sister Cecilia but took Tamsin into my arms. Holding her began to calm me. When I looked down at Tamsin, I saw a fine silver chain around her neck and hanging from it was this pendant, engraved with her birth date.

At first I didn't recognize that it was half of a broken heart. Then Sister sat down next to me on the bed and explained the significance and told me that she had put a chain with the other half of the heart pendant on Tamsin's sister. Like Tamsin's, it was engraved with her birthdate, 6-14-53. She penned a note to be given to the adoptive parents (neither she nor any of the other nuns knew who they were or ever saw them) explaining that the pendant was a gift from the baby's birth mother. It was such a generous, loving thing for her to do. When Tamsin died, I thought about letting the pendant go with her but decided I would keep it. In a way, it represents a bond to both Tamsin and her sister who, hopefully, has the other pendant."

After Tamsin's death, Ellen remained living at St. Gerard's for a few months. The Mother Superior encouraged her to get back out into the world and used her considerable contacts to help Ellen find a good job that would provide the means for her to move on with her life. Ellen got a position on the staff of a local city library branch, not far from St. Gerard's. Over the ensuing years and then decades, Ellen worked in various positions in the New York City library system, ultimately retiring as a research director. She remained in contact with her friends at St. Gerard's and volunteered there off-and-on for many years, working with young unwed mothers, including tutoring them in reading, writing, and arithmetic to help prepare them for life after they gave birth – whether or not they intended to keep their babies.

"Did the nuns ever encourage you to join the convent?" I asked.

"They didn't but I instinctively knew that option was open to me. They did encourage me to become a Catholic. I was raised without religion you see. It's not that my parents were atheists. They were backwoods, rural people who scraped by as their own parents had done. Life was focused on the practicalities of survival, day-by-day. Sunday was a work day like any other. Anyway, when the twins were born, I wanted them to have God's blessings. I took instructions with the Mother Superior. The twins and I were all baptized together. It is one of my most precious memories. The hardest part was my first confession. It was the only time I spoke about what happened with my stepfather Ernie . . . until now."

"Ellen," I said, "did you ever ask the Mother Superior about Tamsin's twin sister, especially after you lost Tamsin? You had such a close relationship with her and she must have known how you longed to know where your daughter was."

Ellen smiled. "Only once, not long after Tamsin's death. She told me that the adoption interview and selection process was handled by a committee under the management of the Diocese. To prevent any possible leak of that confidential information, no one at any of the homes for unwed mothers, even the Mother Superiors, had access to adoption records. At the time, I wasn't sure I believed her; God forgive me for accusing a nun of prevarication. In any case, I had no choice but to accept what she told me and I knew that both my daughters were forever lost to me."

Impetuously taking a leap straight into what should have been a measured, cautious subject of discussion, I asked Ellen if she had ever tried to find her daughter on her own. She had not. I immediately suggested she do the same DNA test that I had done. I explained how it worked, what might be discovered, and why I decided to do it. I offered to order the test kit for her and to take care of the necessary computer interaction related to the results and the review of any familial matches that were identified.

"We can work through it together," I said. "I would love to have a partner on this journey. Better to face it together than alone."

For a few moments she said nothing and I was afraid she would say no, unwilling to add any more chapters to the story she had finally let escape from its Pandora's box. I parted my lips, preparing to apologize for intruding into something so very personal but before I spoke, she did.

A spark of her innate resilience lit her eyes. "Yes, Caitríona, let's do it!"

19. The Proof is in the Pudding

The test kit for Ellen was ordered and arrived in no time. Now a veteran of the 'spit in the tube' process, I cheered Ellen on as she labored to muster and deposit enough of her saliva to reach the designated fill line on the tube, warning her that bubbles did not count toward a successful effort. Ellen tried not to laugh in response and, in between spits, simply said: "Sweet Jesus, just don't put this up on that YouTube thing!"

The results of my own test arrived about three weeks before Ellen's results. Both of us tested as nearly 100% European, my composition pointing primarily to Ireland and Ellen's a combination of Ireland and Great Britain, the British part likely pointing to some family roots in Scotland, something her mother had told her about. Having had no surprising revelations when we saw the ethnicity pie charts resulting from our DNA analyses, we moved on to review the information on each of our DNA matches, a list of others who had taken the DNA test and shared some level of results in common with each of us. My list had over two hundred people listed as possible relatives. Ellen's had over three hundred names.

Before my swan dive on black ice, I had ordered a new copy of my birth certificate as a first step in trying to find out who I really was. The only copy I had was given to me by Nora when I needed it to apply for a Social Security card when I was in high school and got my first part-time job. It was marked *delayed filing*, something I never gave a thought to at the time. It listed Moira as my mother but the name of the father was blank. After Father Aloysius's visit and the news I was adopted, I had pulled it out and seeing that notation again, I was both curious and suspicious about why the reporting of my birth had been delayed. I went on-line and placed an order for another copy of my birth certificate, specifically asking that there be a search for an earlier filing at the time of my birth. Several weeks later, an envelope from the state vital statistics department arrived and I tore it open to find another copy of the same delayed filing birth record I already had.

After that disappointing dead-end, I turned to the DNA testing, hoping for a breakthrough. As I pulled up the list of my newly-discovered DNA relatives I had a knot in my stomach. Surely, with over two hundred possibilities, something would click. I hit the button to 'sort by strength of relationship,' the screen blinked, and up came the list of some 250 people, the closest matches at the top of the list, each match indicating the projected familial relationship (mother, sister, first cousin, second cousin, etc.). I was too pessimistic to have hoped for a 'mother' match but I was praying for at least an aunt, sibling, or first cousin match. No such luck. The closest matches were '4th to 6th cousin' and '5th to 8th cousin.'

I had done a little research about what ancestor 4th cousins share and found that they would have a set of great-great-great-grandparents in common. Considering that each of us has sixteen pairs of great-great-great-grandparents (meaning 32 individual grandparents), the term 'finding a needle in a haystack' seemed woefully inadequate to describe what I was up against. So, another dead-end, for now anyway. More and more people are participating in genealogical DNA testing. Maybe soon one of them would unlock my family history.

After striking out with my DNA results, I started worrying that when Ellen's results came in, she could suffer the same disappointment. Actuarially speaking, I had more time to wait for that *someone* who would take the test and give me the answers I wanted so badly. Ellen was two decades older than me. Time was not on her side. Having been the one she confided in and the one who urged her to take the DNA test, I felt accountable for the outcome. When I finished going through my DNA matches with no new clues to my background, I gently explained my lack of success to Ellen, thinking I should prepare her in case her results also disappointed.

When the list of Ellen's DNA matches was posted, I repeated what I had done with my own results, sorting her DNA relatives by the strength of the projected relationship. Once again I clicked, the screen refreshed, and up came the list. I immediately saw that Ellen's results were very different from my own. The first of the over three hundred matches was for a female and the relationship was labeled as 'parent/child.' I did the same thing that lottery winners do when their winning numbers are announced: I looked at the information multiple times to be sure I had it right. I did. Ellen had a match that could only be the daughter she gave up for adoption, Tamsin's twin sister. Ellen's 'baby' would now be a woman of sixty-two. I could hardly believe it.

Over another of our cups of tea, I told Ellen the news. She was stunned. Then came the questions. *Was I sure?* I answered that I was sure what the results meant and assumed the DNA analysis was reliable. *Is there a name and address for her?* I explained that there wasn't but there was a private communication system through the testing company website that allowed participants to contact each other. *What if she doesn't respond?* I told Ellen the fact that her daughter participated in the testing was an indication she was also searching for answers.

I asked if I could send a message to the woman right away and, of course, Ellen's answer was a resounding 'yes.' I signed on using my laptop, typed the following message and hit the send button:

Hello, I am writing on behalf of my friend Ellen whose DNA test results show a close familial match to you, specifically a parent/child relationship. My friend is in search of her daughter, born in June 1953, who she reluctantly gave up for adoption as she was not able to care for her and provide the home her baby daughter deserved. Ellen is hoping that you will be willing to talk and hopes so much that you are her daughter. We can talk using this message system or, if you like, I can give you my email address or telephone number.

Once that was done, it was a waiting game . . . a nail-biter and emotional rollercoaster. I'm not one to look skyward and ask God for favors despite my Catholic-saturated upbringing but this time, for Ellen's sake, I actually said a prayer or two. Dear God, I prayed, please let the DNA match result be right and please reunite Ellen and her daughter.

20. Knock, Knock, Who's There?

In just hours (it seemed a lot longer to Ellen and me), a response came back including a name, Maria Elena, a phone number, and equally strong hopes that Ellen was indeed her mother. It's hard to explain how quickly a rapport was established, conversations flowed freely, and ties were rewoven between these two people separated for six decades. It reminded me of how close friends who fall out of contact and years later cross paths again describe that experience: their intimate connection seemed to pick up exactly where it left off, as if mere days, rather than years, had passed. After multiple calls during which they exchanged information about themselves and their lives, Maria Elena asked if she could come to see Ellen. Of course the answer was an enthusiastic yes and, just a few weeks later, Maria Elena was to make the long trip from Louisiana to New York.

I was with Ellen when the knock came at her door. She had gotten her hair done and was impeccably dressed as usual. I noticed the silver chain with the broken heart pendant was not hidden under her clothing and I knew she was hoping to see its matching half worn by Maria Elena. I opened the door to Ellen's apartment to find not one but three people: a slim, attractive woman of about sixty, a man of about the same age, and a younger woman perhaps in her late twenties. No doubt seeing the look of surprise on my face (and Ellen's), the older woman spoke.

"Hello, I'm Maria Elena and this is my husband James and our daughter Melanie. I hope you don't mind that I didn't come alone. We were all so anxious to meet you and Melanie insisted she be here."

Ellen and I were momentarily speechless as we processed the fact that she had not only found her daughter but had a granddaughter as well. After a short but awkward silence, we got hold of ourselves and excitedly welcomed them in. It was a glorious day for all of them and their overflowing joy pulled me in and enveloped me as well. After all the initial chatter and warp-speed exchanges that came with catching up and getting to know each other, we enjoyed some of Ellen's favorite tea served with fresh scones I had picked up for the occasion. It was then that I saw Melanie staring at the pendant Ellen was wearing.

"Mom," she said, "look at Grandmother's necklace."

I saw Ellen's eyes slowly close in what I was sure was an expression of the rapture she felt at being called 'grandmother' for the first time. As she had done with me, she lifted the chain and extended the pendant away from her bodice to give the others a better look at it. She had not yet told Maria Elena about her twin sister Tamsin as it didn't seem the kind of thing to tell someone over the phone. Thinking Maria Elena would be alone when she came to meet her, Ellen had planned to tell her about Tamsin and explain how Tamsin's situation had been the reason she had given Maria Elena up for adoption. While Ellen was still struggling with how she would now tell all three of them about Tamsin, Melanie reached beneath the neck of her sweater and pulled out a silver chain. Hanging from the chain was the other half of the broken heart pendant. Actually seeing it after so many years overwhelmed Ellen and she began to weep.

It took a while for Ellen to regain her composure and then slowly tell her daughter, son-in-law, and granddaughter about Tamsin. Ellen recounted the birth of her twin daughters, the realization that Tamsin was disabled, and the agonizing decision to give up one daughter to a better life so the other could be cared for as needed and deserved. She described Tamsin almost poetically, her loving words all but bringing that child alive for those who were hearing about Tamsin for the first time.

"Did we look just alike?" asked Maria.

"No dear," Ellen said. "You were fraternal twins, not identical. Tamsin was fair with blue eyes like me. You look like your father."

"I know," Maria replied.

"Did you say you know you look like your father?" Ellen asked, her face clearly showing her confusion.

"Yes," Maria said. "I didn't intend to tell you about this today but it slipped out and I guess it's my turn to come clean."

Unbelievably, when Maria took the DNA test four years earlier, her closest match was a female projected to be her aunt. Maria jumped to the conclusion that she had found her mother's sister. In fact, she had found a sister of her father – Mateo Soto's older sister Rosa. Rosa had agreed to do the DNA testing at the urging of her granddaughter who was an avid genealogy buff. Maria and Rosa's granddaughter were soon exchanging emails and then phone calls. Ultimately, they agreed there was no doubt that Maria must be Mateo's daughter, a child born of his love for a young woman named Mary Ellen Stuart who he had met during an apple-picking season in West Virginia in the fall of 1952 when he was seventeen.

Ellen was dumbstruck. I let out a small gasp and my mouth worked without uttering a word. I recovered first and anxiously asked the question that was hanging in the air. Was Mateo still alive? He was. He had married in his thirties and lost his wife and their baby in childbirth just a year later. He never married again and thought he had lost the only child he would ever have. When Rosa arranged for Maria to meet him four years ago, he was suspicious at first and openly resistant to the idea that she was his daughter.

"He was polite but distant," Maria explained. "He had lost so much in his life that he was not willing to expose himself to more sorrow. I didn't push. I gave him time and kept in touch with Rosa and her granddaughter Cara. Cara convinced him to do the DNA test himself and when the results came back, there was no longer any reason for him to have doubts. I will never forget how he embraced me the next time I saw him. He told me that when I said my name was Maria Elena, basically a Spanish spelling of your name, Mary Ellen, he thought I was scamming him, somehow having found out about you and using that to fool him for some unsavory purpose."

"Well," I said, "it is a strange coincidence that your name is essentially the same as Ellen's actual given name."

"No, it's not a coincidence at all," explained Maria Elena. "When I was given to my adoptive parents, there was an envelope pinned to my blanket. It contained the broken heart necklace and a short note asking that the necklace be kept for me as a token of affection from my birth mother. The note also requested that I be named Maria Elena if possible."

Maria smiled at Ellen and continued. "My parents . . . my adoptive parents . . . honored both requests. When I was old enough to understand, they showed me the necklace and the note and explained that I was adopted, a gift from God as they were unable to have children of their own. They are both gone now and my only sorrow is that they were not alive to meet the two people who gave me life."

Ellen had not uttered one word since Maria had told us she had found Mateo and he was still alive and now part of her life. I put my hand over hers and squeezed lightly. She looked up into my eyes and her tears came again. Melanie was at Ellen's side in a second and held Ellen's other hand tenderly.

"Grandmother," Melanie said. "I hope those are tears of joy because we are the luckiest family ever. I know Grandpa Mateo will be thrilled to see you. He told us all about you, his first true love. He never forgot about you."

"What must he have thought of me . . . running out on him so suddenly with no explanation?" Ellen said.

"Why, until I came into his life a few years ago, he was sure you had died in the fire," Maria said.

"Fire, what fire?" Ellen asked.

"The fire that destroyed your family's cabin," Maria said. "Your stepfather's body was found near the front door but the rest of the house was all but incinerated and it was assumed you had died in the fire. All those years he mourned your tragic death and I know he always felt the loss of you."

Ellen explained that she had run away after a brutal fight with her stepfather over Mateo and, unable to find Mateo and fearing for his safety, had fled the area in panic. She had no idea that there had been a fire after she left. When she discovered she was pregnant, she knew she could never return home to Callaway and expected that Mateo and his family had moved on as the picking season was over. She had no way to contact him, even if she had wanted to. There was no sense in looking back she explained. She had to move forward and did that with the invaluable support she received from Margot Addison and the nuns of St. Gerard's Home for Unwed Mothers.

In the midst of this incredible sharing of stories and baring of souls, something suddenly occurred to me. Ellen's stepfather Ernie's body had been found *near the door* of his burned out home . . . not near the hearth where he fell motionless after Ellen struck him as he attacked her. Ellen hadn't killed him. Perhaps in his stupor, he had accidentally started the fire and then tried unsuccessfully to escape the inferno. All that mattered was that Ellen was not a murderer as she had feared, even believed, for over sixty years.

21. Parting is Such Sweet Sorrow

Before they left to return to home to Louisiana, Maria Elena, her husband, and daughter Melanie went with Ellen to visit Tamsin's grave. Ellen's journey that had started when she boarded the bus for New York had come full circle. The identity that Ellen had abandoned, Mary Ellen Stuart, would be resurrected and a woman who had lived as a solitary soul and expected to remain so all the days of her life would no longer be alone.

I had once asked Ellen why she never married. I may have asked the question less bluntly but, however I phrased it, I had asked. Her answer was almost identical to Maria's explanation of Mateo's reluctance to believe she was his daughter. She had said Mateo 'had lost so much in his life that he was not willing to expose himself to more sorrow.' Ellen's heart was also awash in loss and without capacity for more sorrow or disappointment.

I was not surprised when Ellen told me Maria had invited her to come to Louisiana. In fact, she asked Ellen to seriously consider relocating there. It was a big decision, not the least of which was the prospect of seeing Mateo once again after so many years. Ellen took her time deciding and first only agreed to a visit. The visit went very well as did her reunion with Mateo who was elated to see her again after believing her dead for so long. After multiple visits to Louisiana, Ellen was ready to make the move to join her family in Louisiana for good. I was sure she had made the right decision and I told her so.

As Ellen's reconnection with her family unfolded, I asked her if I could tell Nicola the whole story. She had no objection. In truth, I was sure that Nic had already put many of the puzzle pieces together. I had dropped some crumbs of information along the way and Nic was very adept at deduction and extremely good at reading me.

As I told Nic the story in detail, she peppered me with questions. Her questions and her logical, sequential thought process actually helped provide context to the story and more clarity for me. Nic said that I might have a new career as a genealogical private eye. She reminded me that 'second act' careers were all the rage according to the popular women's magazines. I countered by saying that if I was to be Sherlock, I would expect her to take on the role of Watson. In fact, our first case as Sherlock and Watson came about not long after we had jested about it.

We went over to help Ellen with her packing for the move to Louisiana. She wanted to weed through her things and figure out what she needed (or just wanted) to take with her, what could be donated to charity, and what should find its way to the trash. She lived a pretty spare existence so there was little for the trash. There were some clothes (in near-perfect condition) and some knick-knacks that were packed up for donation to the local St. Vincent de Paul thrift store. Being a former librarian and a lover of the written word, she did have a lot of books. Going through those took the lion's share of the effort to get her ready for the move.

For quite a while, I had wanted to show her a book of my own. It was my early copy of Thomas Hardy's book, *Tess of the D'Urbervilles*. The first time I visited Ellen's apartment I had seen a copy of that same book on her nightstand. My copy had a particular significance that I wanted to tell her about. On my thirteenth birthday, about five years after my '*mother*' Moira had died, Nora had given me that book. She opened the front cover and showed me an inscription on the blank first page that preceded the title page of the book. It read:

To my precious girl from your loving mother. You are always with me, deep within my heart.

Nora told me the book was a gift from my mother, something to remind me how much she had loved me. Of course I took Nora to mean it was from Moira. At the time I had not an inkling that I had any other mother. I had found it an odd legacy to receive from Moira. Moira wasn't much of a reader – Nora was the one who loved books – and, except for the very early years when Moira would read me bedtime stories, I couldn't recall us ever talking about or sharing a book. Just the same, that book was precious to me. Not only did I read the story countless times since that day when Nora gave me the book, I memorized the inscription and often called it to mind, especially on my birthdays.

After Nora died, while going through her things, I found a note from Moira to Nora marking a page in Nora's well-worn bedside prayer book. It appeared to be half of a small thank-you card, signed by Moira and said:

From my heart, I will always be grateful for all you have done for me and Caitríona. Your loving sister, Moira.

Perhaps because I had just found out that I was adopted, something clicked. I almost ran to pull out my copy of *Tess of the D'Urbervilles* and opened it to the page with the inscription. I laid the torn half of the thank-you note on that page, just under the inscription. My eyes darted back and forth comparing the script, especially the formation of the words both had in common: *heart, loving, always, you, me.* Even if I had wanted to conclude that the same person wrote both, the slant of the handwriting, one flowing gracefully forward and the other leaning backward at a sharp angle, left no doubt that the two were written by different women.

At that moment, I began to believe – moreover to hope, to pray – that the inscription in my book was written by my biological mother and the book was *her* gift to me, not Moira's.

After a few hours of packing with Ellen, we took the expected afternoon tea break. I reached into my tote and pulled out my copy of *Tess of the D'Urbervilles*. I told Ellen and Nic the whole story including how and when I got the book, what I was told by Nora, and my realization that the inscription was not written by Moira. I opened the book and showed them both the inscription and the note card fragment and asked what they thought about the two handwritings. Nic piped up right away and said there was no way the same person wrote them. Ellen reached for the book and, rather than scrutinizing the script, focused on the upper right corner of the page. The corner was torn and had a ragged edge. At that edge were two faint letters that appeared to have been part of a stamp, perhaps the name of a former owner of the book. Ellen passed her finger over those two stamped letters: *ST*. Her face suddenly pale, she looked up and said:

"This book came from the small library at St. Gerard's Home for Unwed Mothers. One of my responsibilities at St. Gerard's was taking donated books, stamping them **ST. GERARD'S** and then adding them to the bookshelves. I would know that green stamp anywhere."

Part Five:

Caitriona

22. Redeeming Green Stamps

After the initial shock of finding out that my book had once been in the stacks at St. Gerard's, my brain was on overdrive as I thought about what that discovery could mean to my search for my birth mother. Ellen had blasted a hole in the brick wall concealing my identity. My optimism returned in full force.

I wasn't the only one running through the new possibilities. Ellen had plans to visit Sister Cecilia before leaving for Louisiana. Sister Cecilia, eighty-six years old, was retired from active religious service and lived in her order's local mother house. Ellen had never lost touch with Sister Cecilia over the years and was anxious to see her friend before moving away. Now that my book had been connected to St. Gerard's, Ellen asked me to go with her to see Sister Cecilia.

"We must tell Cecilia about the book," Ellen said. "In fact, you must bring it with you and show it to her. She was at St. Gerard's for many years and may have information or recollections that can help you figure out if you were one of the St. Gerard's babies."

Ellen didn't have to ask me twice. I couldn't wait to meet Sister Cecilia. When we arrived at the mother house, we were greeted cordially and escorted into a small parlor. Sister Cecilia soon joined us there. Petite and frail-looking, she was wheeled in by a young woman, possibly a postulant or novice, and I saw portable oxygen apparatus peeking out from a side pocket attached to the wheelchair. Her delicate facial features blossomed when she saw Ellen and her affection for her friend lit her face. Ellen went to her and crouched down, taking the nun's face in her hands and kissing her forehead gently.

"Sister," said Ellen, "you are looking very well today. I brought a dear friend with me to meet you. This is Caitríona. She was the one who encouraged me to do the DNA testing that reunited me with my daughter. Caitríona only recently found out that she herself was adopted and I don't think it will surprise you to hear that she has hopes of finding her own biological family. Just days ago, Caitríona showed me a book, inscribed with a note from her mother . . . her birth mother we believe. When I looked at the inscription, I noticed the faded remnant of an ink stamp in the upper right corner of the page and recognized it. I am sure it is the stamp we used to mark books in the library at St. Gerard's."

The elderly nun listened attentively as Ellen talked. On cue, I pulled my book out of my bag, opened to the inscribed page, and handed the book to Sister Cecilia. She examined the page, first reading the inscription and then focusing on the stamped letters *ST*. For a minute or two she said nothing and kept her eyes fixed on the page. I wondered if seeing it had recalled a memory to her or if she might actually say she didn't agree that the stamped letters connected my book to St. Gerard's.

"*Tess of the d'Urbervilles: A Pure Woman Faithfully Represented*," she said, repeating the book's full title. "Such a fine work albeit a sad, uncompromising portrayal of a young woman's tragic life. Hardy had a gift for capturing all aspects of human nature, both native and learned, and revealing the best and worst of his characters in their own environments. The story of Tess and the two men whose flaws and failures doomed her has always been my favorite of all his morality plays."

I was entranced by her words, almost forgetting why we were there and ready to tell her how much I also loved Thomas Hardy's work. Ellen was more attuned to the business of things and drew the conversation back to the hoped for confirmation that the stamp in my book was indeed the one used by St. Gerard's.

"Cecilia," asked Ellen gently, "do you agree that this book was once in the library at St. Gerard's?"

"Oh, no doubt about that," the nun replied. "Those two letters are definitely part of our old green ink stamp."

"I know it's ages ago but do you have any recollection of any of the mothers being especially interested in this book . . . or the time when the book might have gone missing from the library at St. Gerard's?" asked Ellen.

"Well Ellen, I guess you will have to serve as my confessor when it comes to the answer to that question," said Sister Cecilia. "I do remember the young woman because I was complicit in the disappearance of that book from St. Gerard's."

"How so, Sister?" asked Ellen.

"Well, Ellen, if you remember, I was just months past having taken my final vows when you came to St. Gerard's. While I was ecstatic at officially being a religious, my young head was still full of the remnants of my independent, secular life. Those as yet undisciplined influences led me to do things like writing that note to your daughter's adoptive parents, enclosing the broken heart necklace and audaciously suggesting that they name the baby Maria Elena – an homage to her father's ethnicity of course. Believing that I had gotten away with that, I tried something similar with the young Irish girl and her baby daughter. Seeing her shyness and knowing she must be very homesick, I had encouraged her to take advantage of our little library, saying it would help with her English language abilities. Sometimes I would sit with her and talk about the books she read. She was very moved by *Tess of the D'Urbervilles*, very moved. I expect she identified with Tess, a naive young woman who finds herself pregnant and alone.

When the Irish girl's baby was born and it came time for the adoption, she was terribly overwrought. She would pace the room, holding that book in her hand. That's when I got another brainstorm. I suggested we send the book with her baby, asking the adoptive parents keep it for the child as a token of her birth mother. I told her to write a short note to her daughter on the first page."

"It was your idea . . . you who were responsible for me having this book?" I asked.

"Well, assuming you are her daughter - and I pray that you are - then, yes, it was my doing," said the nun. "That was the last time I did anything like that. The day after that baby left St. Gerard's, Mother Superior summoned me to her office. I was in big trouble. Not only did she know about the book I had sent with that baby, she was also well aware of my having sent the necklace and note with Ellen's daughter. She threatened me with expulsion if I ever did anything like that again. I was shaking in my boots. I never knew until now that, in both cases, she did not undo what I had done. I assumed she had confiscated the note and necklace and also the copy of *Tess of the D'Urbervilles*. Obviously she did not.

Now she's left me to wonder and hypothesize why she didn't. That seems a fitting punishment for my impulsive actions and I expect Mother Superior would agree."

Ellen breathed in audibly and I expected she was thanking God that Mother Superior didn't foil Sister Cecilia's plotting. In an even tone, she asked Sister Cecilia to tell us about the young Irish girl in as much detail as she could remember. Cecilia nodded in agreement. I felt the rhythm of my heart suddenly change as anxiety mixed with excitement and washed over me.

"She was a mere slip of a girl, perhaps sixteen years old, with long wavy very dark brown hair. That head of hair all but overwhelmed her small face and frame. She was very shy, almost skittish when she arrived at St. Gerard's. She was so far from home, you see. She had come from Ireland, apparently sent away to try and conceal the shame of her pregnancy."

"Sent the child all the way from Ireland to America," Ellen said quietly. "That seems an especially extreme reaction to a teenage pregnancy, even for Ireland in those times."

"I believe there was some kind of family or other close connection between the girl's people and our Mother Superior who herself was born in Ireland," explained Cecilia. "Both the girl and Mother Superior were Irish-speakers and, more than once, I came upon them speaking to each other in their native tongue."

I could not keep from interrupting. "Sister, what was that young woman's name? Do you remember?"

"She was introduced to us as Delia. That could have been her actual name but it was also commonly used as a pet name for girls named Bridget."

"Do you remember her last name?" I asked.

"I don't, beyond the impression that it was a common Irish surname," said Cecilia.

Ellen was way ahead of me in the formation and sequencing of new questions for Sister Cecilia. I thanked God that both Ellen and Sister Cecilia were still as sharp as tacks.

"Cecilia," said Ellen, "perhaps Delia was from the same part of Ireland, even the same location, as Mother Superior. Do you know where Mother Superior was from in Ireland?"

"I don't recall," said the nun. "Mother Superior was inclined to be very closed-mouth, not one to talk about herself. I wasn't sure if that was because she was just naturally a private person or if she felt she needed to maintain a distance between herself and her charges."

"Maybe we could talk to your Mother Superior," I interjected.

"No dear, Mother Superior went to her reward a decade ago," said the nun.

"How stupid of me," I said. "Of course she's gone by now."

"Not stupid dear," said the nun. "One of my housemates is ninety-eight years old. Mother Superior succumbed to cancer or she might very well have been here to answer your questions."

"Is there anyone else still around from the days when I first met you at St. Gerard's?" asked Ellen. "Perhaps someone from the Diocese or the adoption committee? I assume that Monsignor Winstead has also passed away."

"Yes Ellen, the Monsignor passed away some years ago. Rumor has it that he is now bellowing at the saints and angels in similar fashion to the way he did on earth when he was our diocesan administrator."

Ellen and I laughed out loud at that quip. It seemed that the Mother Superior's admonishments had not completely reined in Sister Cecilia's tendency to be a free-thinking independent force. Seeing that she was looking a bit fatigued and had glanced down toward her portable oxygen, we rose to leave, thanking her with gentle hugs and kisses. She was such a precious person.

As we walked down the sidewalk toward my car, I thanked Ellen for all her efforts and for the opportunity to meet Sister Cecilia. I asked if she thought it would be alright if I visited Sister Cecilia again – not to talk about the woman I now believed to be my mother – but to discuss Thomas Hardy's books. Ellen said she was certain Cecilia would welcome that and the talk would no doubt be lively.

As we approached my car, a voice called out to Ellen. We turned to see the young woman who had admitted us to the mother house coming toward us. She caught up to us and, a bit breathless, said she had a message for us from Sister Cecilia.

"Sister said you should go to see Father Al at St. Columba's. She said that when he was a young priest, he served as secretary to Monsignor Winstead for a number of years. He may be able to answer your questions or be of some other assistance to you."

23. The Case of the Premonitory Priest

Nic and I took Ellen to the airport to catch her flight to New Orleans. I knew I was going to miss her very much. As she stepped up onto the sidewalk at the terminal and walked toward the doors, she turned once more to smile at us.

"Make sure we get an invite to your wedding," Nicola called to her with a big smirk on her face.

"Of course dear," said Ellen. "At my age the possible choices for bridesmaids are limited. I'll being needing both of you I'm sure. How does something in pink with lots of ruffles and lace sound for your dresses?"

As she turned away, she left us laughing. We hoped she would marry Mateo. Why not? Wedding or no, we had every intention of making a trip to Louisiana before too long to visit Ellen and her new family but, first, we had some pressing business right here at home. As I drove us home from the airport neither of us had much to say. When I dropped Nicola off, she shut the car door but then quickly reopened it, leaning in to look at me.

"Well Sherlock," she said, "when are we going to see the priest?"

"Why, as soon as I can get an appointment with him, my dear Watson," I replied. "There's no time to waste and I'm up for a good old-fashioned inquisition, especially when it involves Father Aloysius."

Yes, Father Al, once the young secretary to Monsignor Winstead, was none other than Nora's confidant, Father Aloysius. It was time to find out what other secrets the good Father had accumulated over the last half-century. I called the parish office, spoke with the secretary and made an appointment to see Father Aloysius the following afternoon.

Nicola and I were shown into Father Aloysius's small private office upon arrival at the rectory. The pleasant aroma wafting from the kitchen blended with the distinct scent of pipe tobacco in Father's office. Father joined us a few minutes later looking a bit surprised to see that I had someone with me. He sat down behind his desk, folded his hands, looked at me, and asked why I had come to see him.

"I suspect you know why, Father," I said.

"I'm not sure I do," he replied. "Are you or your friend in need of counseling perhaps?"

"No Father," I said. "I . . . we . . . are in need of information. We have reason to believe that you can provide the information we need or, if necessary, direct us to someone else who can. When you came to my house to deliver the note from Nora, you offered to talk with me after I read it if I liked. Well, here I am. My friend Nicola is fully aware of the contents of Nora's letter so no need to worry about talking in front of her."

"I see," said the priest. "Well, how can I help?"

I pulled out my copy of *Tess of the D'Urbervilles*, read the inscription out loud, and then told him how Nora gave me the book on my thirteenth birthday saying it was inscribed to me by my mother. I moved right on to say I was certain that the woman who wrote the inscription was not Moira and suspected the book came from my birth mother. He had not said a word to that point and so I paused to give him an opportunity to comment. When he did not, I went on, enumerating the clues we had discovered and, like Sherlock Holmes himself, laid out a theory of my birth and adoption. I finished with a direct volley, asking him to confirm that my mother was Delia, the young woman from Ireland.

"Caitríona, some things are better left alone," was his response. "I feel I must caution you that going down this road will likely only bring you disappointment and even pain."

"More pain than finding out at age sixty that I was adopted?" I asked. "More disappointment than discovering that a woman I thought was my loving aunt deceived me for decades and then, from her grave, dropped the truth on me like a bomb?"

"She loved you deeply whether she was your aunt or not. In fact, she loved you as a mother loves her child. She gave up her own life to care for your mother . . . Moira I mean . . . and you. She always put you and Moira first," he said.

"You seem very tuned in to Nora, Father," I said sarcastically. "I noticed, a long time ago, that you and Nora were unusually cozy. Just what were you two up to . . . beyond deceiving me?"

"Cat!" said Nicola sharply. "I know you're hurt and angry but it won't help to browbeat Father Aloysius. We're looking for his help."

I wheeled around toward her but the look of concern on her face stopped me from lashing out at her. I took a breath, calming myself and turned my gaze back to Father Aloysius, a slight man in his eighties with a full head of gray hair and smoky blue eyes that remained fixed on me.

"Will you help me?" I asked in a conciliatory tone. "I accept responsibility for whatever consequences may come from learning what you know about the circumstances of my birth. I won't give up on this, even if you refuse to help me so, please, don't hold back and force me to struggle on for God knows how long when you could help. You won't be hurting any of the people you have protected for so long. Moira, Nora, Monsignor Winstead, Mother Superior – they're all dead and gone and, most likely, my birth parents are as well. If Nora didn't want me to know the truth, she wouldn't have left the note for me and, frankly, if you were hell-bent on keeping this secret, you could have destroyed the note rather than delivering it to me."

Father Aloysius raked his hands through his hair, put both elbows on the desk and then slowly lowered his head and rested it on his palms. For a few minutes he did not speak and I worried that I had pushed him too hard. He finally lifted his head, picked up his pipe, lit it, took a drag, and then focused his blue-gray eyes on me.

"Caitríona," he said exhaling a puff of smoke, "I will tell you everything I know but, once again, I advise you to tread carefully. The road to the past is often littered with shards and fragments of fractured lives, some of those later healed or redeemed, others not."

"As far as my relationship with Nora," he continued, "I'm afraid your years of editing romance and mystery novels have left you with a tendency to flights of fancy and visions of boogeymen around every corner. Nora and I *were* more than priest and parishioner, but not in the way you are suggesting. We were dear friends and confidants and, yes, the original basis of our close connection began with your adoption. I miss Nora as you would miss Nicola should she no longer be on this earth. For a priest, having a true friend, a person of absolute trust, is a rare gift. Nora was that for me and I pray that I was likewise for her. That's all I am going to say on that subject. As for the rest, it will have to wait. I have an appointment in ten minutes. If you come back this evening at seven, I will tell you everything I can."

24. Follow the Yellow Brick Road

"Jesus Christ Cat, you almost killed that old man," Nic said when we got out onto the sidewalk. "Is there some reason you went off on him that way?"

"I guess he's the only one left that I can confront about what was concealed from me," I said. "I didn't realize how angry I was. When he tried to fob me off with those old platitudes about leaving well enough alone, it just triggered me and out it gushed. I hope he comes clean tonight. I have no more patience for games and mental jousting. It's my life, not his or anyone else's."

We arrived back at the rectory promptly at seven that evening, carrying a peace offering: a home-baked red velvet cake. It was Nic's idea, of course. I would have brought a box of Entenmann's. She made me 'help' her bake the cake, just so I could tell Father Aloysius that *I* had made it. I don't bake but I made the best of it, dipping my finger into the sweet, creamy icing every time Nic turned her back. Not sure that cake was the best weapon to ensure Father Aloysius's complete cooperation, I picked up a bottle of Jameson's. We were going in armed to the teeth.

We handed the cake and the Jameson's over to the housekeeper when she answered the door and asked if she could serve it with some tea or coffee in a half-hour or so. She nodded her agreement and disappeared into the kitchen after showing us to the parlor. It was a homey room with some vintage religious prints of Jesus and Mary on the walls and a small fireplace flanked by identical bookshelves. There were some old framed photos on the mantle and above that hung a framed proclamation with a photo of Pope John Paul II. I laid the pen and pad I had brought with me on the small coffee table in front of the sofa. I was ready to take written notes to make sure I didn't forget anything Father Aloysius told me.

Father came in looking more relaxed than we had left him hours before. He had already heard about the red velvet cake we brought and joked that although a bribe was not necessary, sweets were always happily accepted. When Nicola told him that I made the cake, an imagine of Nora flashed in my minds-eye wagging her finger and threatening to wash Nic's mouth out with soap for lying to a priest.

After those preliminaries, we got down to business. I asked Father to take us back to the beginning when he first heard about or met Delia, leaving nothing – however minor – out of the story. I picked up my pad and pen anxiously, determined not to miss anything. With that said, Father Aloysius began to lay down the paving stones that would become the path to my early life. I felt like Dorothy when she found the Wizard of Oz, the person she believed could make it possible for her to return home.

According to Father Aloysius, Delia was indeed my birth mother. Sister Cecilia's recollection of Delia as a very young 'slip of a girl' matched Father Aloysius's description of her. Delia was sent to St. Gerard's from Ireland and, although not openly acknowledged, Father believed Delia was a relation of some kind to the Mother Superior. He remembered that Delia's last name was Doherty.

I punctuated his narrative with clarifying questions. I asked if he knew where in Ireland the Mother Superior had lived before coming to America. He recalled that she was from Derry or its surrounds. In fact, she had once asked him to help her wire some money to her brother in Derry.

"Derry?" Nicola asked. "Is that the same as Londonderry?"

"Not to the people who live there," Father Aloysius retorted. "In fact, yes, both names refer to the same city in Northern Ireland."

At that moment, I hadn't a clue what Father was getting at with that offhanded reply. Before I could ask, the housekeeper came in with a tray. She handed each of us a generous slice of cake and a cup of tea. She put the tray on a nearby table. On it were three small sparkling crystal glasses containing a shot of Jameson's. Nicola picked up one of the shot glasses and held it up to the light.

"Father," she said, "these glasses are so delicate and finely made. Looks like you broke out your best for us."

"Well Nicola," he said, "there's a story to those fine little tumblers."

"Of course there would be a story," I said wryly. "Isn't there always a story when you ask an Irishman a question?"

"Ignore her Father," said Nicola. "I want to hear the story."

"Those glasses, a set of six of them that is, were an ordination gift given to me by a group of my parents' friends. I think they are Irish crystal, at least that's what my mother believed. Irish or otherwise, and lovely as they are, they were an impractical gift for a newly-hatched priest. My father called them a 'useless fancy' that the gift givers 'could hardly afford.' Actually, I think my father's attitude about the glasses was a manifestation of his frustration over my becoming a priest. He wanted me to become a teamster longshoreman and works the docks, a job he believed would be secure and, by the standards of those days, financially lucrative. My mother, on the other hand, was bursting with pride when I said I wanted to enter the religious life. They had more than one row over the whole thing. Over the years a few of the glasses fell victim to drops and poor packing when I moved parishes. These three survive."

The tale of the fancy glasses retold, Father Aloysius got back to my story. It came out in small waves as if memories were lapping at the shores of his brain. Sometimes he would pause for several minutes and I thought he was at the end of what he had to say but then he would resume talking.

As for the circumstances that had brought Delia to St. Gerard's, her banishment from Ireland, while largely owing to her being pregnant and unwed, was apparently further fueled by the identity of the man who fathered her baby. Father Aloysius, then working as secretary to Monsignor Winstead, understood that the baby's father was from a republican family and locals suspected he was a member of the IRA. He explained that while Delia's Catholic family may have had republican sympathies, having their daughter involved with an IRA activist would not stand. The need to sever their daughter's ties to a man who would likely become a hunted criminal destined for prison . . . or a premature death . . . was paramount.

"Was part of the plan to give Delia's baby up for adoption?" I asked.

"I understood that Delia, a lovesick seventeen-year-old, wanted to keep the baby but had agreed to leave the infant here temporarily at her parents' insistence," Father said. "She was to return to Ireland so that a plan, a cover story I expect, could be concocted . . . as if everyone in the area didn't know all the dirt about the pregnancy."

"Was Moira recruited to take care of the baby . . . I mean *me*?" I asked.

"Not Moira . . . Nora," he said. "Nora was the one who was asked to take the baby in temporarily."

I said I didn't understand. Father said the next part of the story wouldn't be easy for him to tell and likely difficult for me to hear as it would upend all my beliefs about the two women who raised me. I said, with confidence, that I was sure I wanted to know and couldn't believe it would be any more earth-shaking than finding out about my adoption.

Father began by saying, for Nicola's benefit, that Moira and Nora had been born in Ireland and left there for America after the deaths of both of their parents. Many young native Irish left their homeland in the early 1950s looking for a better life in the States. Nora, five years older than Moira, was very protective of her little sister and with reason.

"The way we used to say it, Moira was 'slow,' a bit 'simple' I mean," said Father. "She was almost childlike in some ways, but not obviously so. She was a young woman of delicate temperament, easily shaken at times. Nora knew exactly how to keep her on an even keel and feeling safe. Nora was utterly devoted to her."

"I don't remember her like that," I said with an edge in my voice.

"You were a young child Caitríona," he said. "You wouldn't have seen it as it wasn't that obvious, especially with Nora managing the situation. I remember visiting at your home on days when Moira was in bed because of one of her headaches. I recall seeing you, not more than five or six years old, sitting at her bedside, gently stroking her hair, trying to relieve her pain. It was not headaches that drove her to her bed, Caitríona. Those were the days when the world was just too much for her to handle because of her fragile nature."

Refusing to admit that I did remember days when Moira stayed in bed and Nora told me to be very quiet as my mother was suffering with a terrible headache, I moved the conversation on, getting back to his statement that Nora was the one meant to be my adoptive mother.

"If all that is true, how did I become Moira's child?"

"From the beginning Moira took on a motherly role with you. She delighted in taking care of you. Since Nora had a job and having you stay with them was supposed to be a temporary arrangement, it made sense for it to go that way," he said. "When you first said 'Mama,' you said it to Moira, she being the one who was most often with you. When Moira died, Nora assumed the role of your mother, the role originally intended for her. Time went on and nothing more was said about Delia or reuniting you with her. We assumed that Mother Superior had contact with Delia or her people in Ireland but she never said. It was, using today's vernacular, a 'don't ask, don't tell' operation. You had a good home and the love of two women who were devoted to you. Case closed."

"So am I to believe that I was not told about my adoption because of some spoken or unspoken agreement in keeping with *don't ask, don't tell*?" I said. "Why tell me at all then? If I had died before Nora, I wouldn't have known, would I? Perhaps she would have blurted it out in a confession at my deathbed in that case. Why drop it on me after her death, upending my world and leaving me without the chance to ask her the questions she must have known I would have? She, better than anyone, knew all I had lost in the accident that took Gemma. Why would she take away the only remaining family I believed I had? It seems so cruel . . . and I never knew her to be cruel."

"She always had misgivings about not telling you the truth," he said, "but had concerns about your ability to handle the truth. You were not a light-hearted child or adolescent. There was an intensity of feeling in your nature that sometimes manifested in moods and withdrawal from others. You weren't the typical child who jumped rope and played hopscotch with the neighborhood kids or the typical teenager giggling with her girlfriends about what boys you liked that week. You were already carrying some kind of weight she would say; no point in adding more to the load."

"So," I asked, "what changed her mind?"

"It was the onset of the dementia," he said. "In the earliest stages, I'm sure you know she was quite aware of what was happening to her and where it would lead. When I visited her one day, she handed me the unsealed envelope and asked that I read the enclosed letter to you. I was truly surprised at what she wanted me to do. I said, 'Why do this after all these years?' She had the answer ready. She said the dementia was slowly robbing her of everything and everyone, more specifically her memories and her family. She said she believed she had no right, whatever the well-intentioned justification, to rob you of your birth family, especially when her death would leave you alone. She said her failing mind had given her a new sense of clarity."

"Did Nora know who my biological parents were and the story of how my mother came to be at St. Gerard's? Nora's letter only told me I was adopted and apologized for keeping that from me. It contained no information about the circumstances of my birth."

"Neither Nora nor Moira knew the truth of your parentage. I knew them through their volunteering and charitable work in the parish and local community. When a temporary home was needed for you, they seemed a perfect fit for the job and were happy to take you in."

"Well," I said as I held back my tears, "as they say, the road to hell is paved with good intentions. Is that all of it?"

"Those are the facts as I know them," Father said. "Although I wasn't able to oblige your romantic imaginings as to the relationship between Nora and me, I feel sure I've now given you plenty of grist, all of it true, to prime your deductive and creative juices."

I asked a few more questions. *What was Mother Superior's name?* It was Sheila Orrin. *Did he know the name of my father?* He did not. *Did he ever hear what became of my mother or my father?* He had not. *Were there any adoption files still in the hands of the Diocese or in some church archive?* He thought not but would make some inquiries.

After a sixty-year delay, the journey back to the beginnings of my life had taken just two hours. Later, a realization came to me. Nora could have left her letter to me with any one of her friends or could have left it in the strong box where she kept her will. Instead, she made Father Aloysius her messenger, insisting that he read the letter before the envelope was sealed. She meant for me to have contact with him because she knew he had the information about my origins that I would be looking for. Well done Nora.

Part Six:

Nicola

25. The Third Leg of the Stool

As I undressed, I looked down at my abdomen sure I would see the telltale hue of yellow, as in 'yellow-bellied coward.' I recognized its lack of muscle tone and the faded scar from a long ago surgery. It was the same pale pouch – not a hint of jaundice. Just the same, my stomach had been rumbling for hours and I felt sure there was some bitter yellow bile in play.

Being party to Ellen and Cat's headlong plunges into the murky waters of family skeleton resurrection had an unexpectedly potent effect on me. I shivered as I imagined them queuing up with members of the Polar Bear Club on a cold January morning for the ritual New Year's Day wading into the icy waters of some beach, unafraid of the potential consequences. Why couldn't I strip down and jump in?

We had barely closed the door of the rectory behind us when Cat shifted gears and began to lay out a strategy for tracking down what became of her Irish outlaw father. Always a quick study, she was becoming quite the genealogical researcher in no time flat. She spent hours at a library branch that had a dedicated family history research room. The director of that genealogy room became Cat's newest BFF, orienting her to the array of available resources including books, directories, and other publications in their stacks and cabinets along with the library's on-line subscription databases such as Ancestry.com and newspaper archives. Cat approached this project as she did every other challenge: all-in and with a mindset that walls were for scaling.

For my part, I couldn't understand how the shelves of a local library or American newspaper archives could hold the key to finding Cat's parents. It seemed her father was never in the States and her mother Delia was here for less than a year, that time spent cloistered at St. Gerard's. Cat explained that sites like Ancestry.com and FamilySearch.org had global family history records and that, as to Ireland, there were specialized sites offering Catholic parish records, early 20th century census records, and even old Irish newspapers. She was determined and optimistic, just the needed combination for such a daunting journey of discovery.

When she announced one day that as soon as she had a 'good lead,' she would be heading for Ireland and expected me to again be Watson to her Holmes, I was speechless. Never saw that coming. She said we should make a real odyssey of it, also spending time in Scotland and maybe a few days in London. I felt my breath catch and my stomach clench. My reaction (really my lack of reaction) caught Cat by surprise. Her brow furrowed and head cocked to the side, she studied me for a moment.

"Wow," she said, "not the reaction I was expecting. Are you that sick of me and my new obsession? I thought it would be an adventure for us. At our age, we should be jazzed that we can take something like this on. Better than bus rides to Atlantic City or Sunday afternoon bingo at St. Columba's, no?"

My reply was forced and unconvincing I'm sure. "Cat, you caught me by surprise, that's all. You know I'm behind you all the way."

"I don't want you behind me," she said. "We're a team. Remember, I'm your emergency contact and you're mine. We even have those matching living wills to prove it."

I knew the jig, my jig that is, was up. I just had to get my head screwed on straight so I could tell Cat the story she should have heard a long time ago. Once I did, Ellen's story, Cat's story and mine would be like the three legs of an old primitive stool I had bought years ago at a flea market in Pennsylvania. Each leg was turned by hand, each one slightly different from the others. All three were necessary, each relying on the others for stability. Once my purge was over, stability would be just what I needed.

"Cat," I said. "Let's put our heads together and make a plan and timeline. We have to be sure you've gathered enough information and specifics so we're heading in the right direction . . . literally. Ireland is a small country but not so small that we can wander around hoping to happen upon someone who is just waiting to tell you about your father and mother."

She agreed. I swear that my having put a framework around her envisioned adventure made her dig in and work even more energetically, if that was possible. She also kept me up-to-date on her progress and even her dead ends. I started to get the bug myself. Doing genealogy research, rattling old skeletons and connecting them to each other actually was detective work.

While Cat kept searching, I started preparing to tell her about my own adventure in Scotland so many years ago, wondering if I could ever go back there again. The lines of the much-loved Scottish anthem *Loch Lomond* came back to me, the tune repeating in loops in my mind.

> *"You'll take the high road and I'll take the low road,*
> *And I'll be in Scotland before you;*
> *But me and my true love will never meet again,*
> *On the bonnie, bonnie banks of Loch Lomond."*

Traditionally, the term 'high road' was interpreted as the path traveled by the living, the 'low road' being the path that brought the spirits of the dead back home. Written in the 1840s, those iconic lyrics could just as well have been written for me in 1969.

26. A Night Without a Morning

Wine? Check. Snacks? Check. Then it must be time for the curtain to go up on tonight's special presentation of *It Happened in Scotland*. That futile attempt to take the edge off with a bit of humor having fallen flat, I took the bottle of merlot, filled my glass and drained most of it. Cat took the bottle, poured for herself, grabbed a piece of cheese and popped it into her mouth. She raised her eyebrows and lifted her chin in my direction as if to say *I'm ready, let's hear it*. She heard it alright . . . for two solid hours punctuated by the polishing off of two bottles of wine and multiple rounds of cheese and crackers.

My story began in 1968 when I headed off for my freshman year of college thanks to a new student loan program created by Congress. The first person in my family to have that opportunity, I envisioned endless possibilities and a life so different from the limited horizons of my parents. It was only a state school here in New York but, to me, it was as good as Harvard or Yale.

I was in the liberal arts program meaning that, depending on your viewpoint, I was either building a well-rounded foundation for my future or I was about to waste four years learning nothing of any importance to the goal of graduating with a career path and marketable skills. Among the menu of courses available to me were several history courses and I had enrolled in an introductory European history class.

One of the additional benefits of the student loan program was job assistance, meaning that students like me were helped to find part-time employment on campus or at nearby businesses. I was happy to juggle a job and my studies, needing the money and believing the work experience would be useful. Perhaps because I was taking that European history class, I was offered a job doing administrative work for the head of the history department. I did a lot of 'errand girl' stuff in the beginning but as the months went by I helped with things that were more interesting. One of those was assisting with the planning of a student exchange program between our school and a small college in Edinburgh, Scotland. I wondered how a small campus like ours could offer an overseas option. Simple explanation: our history department chair had a cousin who was a professor at the Edinburgh school.

No need to go into the weeds to describe how I wangled participation in the next school year's exchange program. Suffice to say I was successful in getting to spend my sophomore year in bonnie Scotland. In just over a year, I had gone from being a high school senior in the suburbs to an international exchange student getting ready to get on a plane for the first time. In order to save the money necessary for the airfare and living expenses in Scotland, I got a summer job back home . . . actually two summer jobs. I waitressed and I worked the ticket window at a local theatre. I was hell-bent on going and I did.

The first time I walked the Royal Mile from Edinburgh Castle to Holyrood Palace I swore I would never go home. I felt transported to another world . . . another time . . . and my feet all but danced on the cobblestones. Walking the streets of old Edinburgh in the shadow of buildings that had stood there for hundreds of years felt strangely like coming home. People had told me I wouldn't like the city, that it was gritty and dark. I found it nothing at all like that. If my interest in history had been lukewarm before, being in Edinburgh turned up the heat. There was so much to see beyond the enormous castle and the palace that was once home to Mary, Queen of Scots: museums, galleries, churches (*kirks* to the Scots), not to mention the iconic statue of the terrier Bobby at the Greyfriars Kirkyard. I spent every spare moment roaming the city and even got a part-time job clerking in a tobacconist shop on the Royal Mile.

When I paused to take a breath, Cat smiled and said "Aha, so that's where you picked up your preference for terriers," a reference to the two dogs I had owned when I met her, both of those sweet boys now gone.

"Yes, Cat," I said. "That's what I wanted to confess. I developed a terrier addiction while studying in Scotland." After a few swallows of wine, I resumed my narrative, thinking that I better pick up the pace if I was going to get to the actual confessional part before the wine took both of us off.

I loved working at the tobacconist and meeting the locals. The sound of their Scottish burr was music to my ears, despite sometimes struggling to understand what was being said to me. When they heard my American accent they were curious and I enjoyed telling them about myself and my life in New York. They were so friendly, the regulars often taking a few extra minutes to ask how my studies were going before wishing me a '*guid day.*'

One evening, hearing the shop door creak open, I looked up to see a tall young man who appeared to be in his mid-twenties smiling in my direction. I took a sudden short, shallow breath followed by a soft gasp I hoped he didn't hear as he approached the counter. He asked if there were any copies of *The Scotsman* left. Still busy gaping at him, I didn't respond. When he moved closer to the counter and asked if I was alright, I snapped out of my trance. I pulled out a copy of *The Scotsman* and handed it to him. He dropped the coins into my palm and I felt the lightest touch of his fingers. When the door closed behind him, I broke into prayer, beseeching God to send him back the next time I was working.

"Wow," Cat said, "he was that good-looking? I can't imagine you swooning over a man."

"Actually," I said, "he wasn't. I can't explain it. He did have striking green eyes but he wasn't handsome in the typical sense of that word. He was tall and lanky, a bit too thin and gangly. He was wearing the customary wool tweed jacket and corduroy slacks when he first came in and was carrying a beat-up leather portfolio. Even now, forty-five years later, I can visualize it."

"So," Cat said, "I guess there's no need to ask if he came back in."

"No need," I said softly.

My instant crush on Alec Campbell, a newly-appointed assistant professor at the University of Edinburgh, didn't fade with his visits to the shop in the days and weeks that followed and, if he didn't come by for his newspaper for several days, I was almost distraught. One evening when he came in, he brought a thermos of hot tea and an extra cup and we sipped tea as we talked. Our conversation was fluid and lively, as if we had known each other for a long time. On a cold, rainy night he came in near closing with the usual thermos and cup. When I locked up, he offered me a ride back to campus. When we got there, I turned to get out and then abruptly turned back toward him and kissed him. He seemed surprised at first but I pressed on – literally – and he was soon kissing me back. The heart and the hormones want what they want and soon enough we were parked in one of the dark side streets and were in the back seat of that old car. It was glorious, everything I wanted it to be. When he dropped me off, I was sure this was it. He was the love of my life – all nineteen years of it.

When he didn't come into the shop for three days, I didn't know what to think. Sick to my stomach, I ran possible explanations for his absence through my mind over and over again. Did I misread his interest in me? Was I too forward – an American floosy up for a one-night stand in the back seat of any guy's car? On the fourth day he came in just before closing time looking very sheepish, no thermos and cup in hand. I could not get him to make eye contact as he stood in front of me obviously trying to muster the courage to say what he wanted to say. He took a deep breath and said the words I would never forget:

Nicola, I am engaged to be married. What we did was a mistake. I love my fiancé Margaret. I can't see you again. I'm sorry.

I had no words to utter in response to his. I felt the tears coming and opened my eyes as wide as possible trying to stave them off. I dared not blink and release a torrent in front of him. When the door closed behind him, I felt a wave of heat rise up inside me and if I hadn't gripped the edge of the counter, I believe I would have collapsed to the floor. I locked up, counted out the till, sat down on the stool behind the counter, and only then wept like a child. To quote Robert Burns:

What is life, when wanting love? A night without a morning...

27. What Child is This?

I held onto the hope that he would come back. He would realize I was the one he was meant to be with. He didn't come back. I asked around, carefully, and found out he was to marry the daughter of one of the administrators at the university where he worked. She was a graduate of the University of Edinburgh herself and also worked on the staff there. They were the very definition of a couple with 'things in common' including a future together. There was no place for an infatuated American teenager in Alec Campbell's life.

I started the slow crawl back to emotional equilibrium, refocusing my energies on academics and looking forward to spending the upcoming holiday season in Scotland. There was no shortage of things *holiday* to partake of including musical events, live theatre, and festivities organized by my school including a Christmas dance. I accepted virtually every invitation extended to me. One of those was to join my Scottish roommate Lorna's family for the Christmas weekend. I checked with the others in our exchange student group before accepting and found that each of us had been invited for at least Christmas dinner with a local family. I happily accepted Lorna's kind offer.

Spending Christmas embedded in a real Scottish household was amazing: the food, the traditions, the warm hospitality, all of it. Taking it in and enjoying myself, I didn't have time to fixate on Alec. The world would go on after all, my own life and future included. I promised myself that the spring term would be a new start for me and I was anxious to savor my remaining time in Edinburgh.

When I got back to the college and was unpacking my small suitcase, I unzipped the side pocket to check for anything I had left in there. I reached in and pulled out a small pouch containing sanitary napkins. That's when it hit me: I had been expecting my period and had brought several napkins with me when I packed for the three days at Lorna's home. At first, in my naiveté, I just thought that with all the upset about Alec, my period was just off-schedule. To say I was inexperienced when it came to sex is a gross understatement. No, Alec wasn't my first. He was my second. The first time was a high school thing that was awkward, fumbling, and over in a couple minutes. The difference was that my high school paramour had come prepared with a condom. He had been carrying it tucked in his wallet for quite a while, ever hopeful that providence would deliver an opportunity to slip it on.

It soon became clear that my period was on hiatus. I was in a panic but couldn't let on to anyone. It was like I was screaming bloody blue murder inside my head where only I could hear it. When the morning sickness came on, all doubts were banished. One thing about not being able to keep food down – it slows down the pregnancy weight gain and helps conceal the situation. I kept myself together for the most part in the initial weeks, estimated when I would be due to deliver, and tried to make a plan for getting medical care (for the baby's sake). Even though it was the 'swinging sixties' and young women back home were going braless, protesting the war in Viet Nam, and experimenting with drugs and sex, that wasn't me. All I could think about was hurting and embarrassing my parents, losing my loan, and flushing my chance to graduate from college.

When I was between three and four months along, I came to a decision. I would have the baby in Scotland and give it up for adoption. Unwed mothers and illegitimate babies being nothing new or uncommon even in bonnie Scotland, it wasn't difficult to find a church-affiliated group that helped support the mothers and place their babies. They referred me to a local doctor and they promised me confidentiality. I hoped for the best.

On the days when my spirit flagged and I felt very low, I toyed with telling Alec about my pregnancy. I pictured him telling me he wanted the baby and would tell his bride-to-be the truth. In some of those daydreams he would say he would break his engagement and be with me. In others, he said he would raise our baby with her, not me. Soon enough I would snap out of it knowing that there wasn't a chance in hell either of those things would happen so there was no point in telling him.

I am sure some people figured out that I was pregnant by the end of the spring semester even though I hadn't gained much weight (by pregnancy standards) but no one asked and I didn't tell. The adoption paperwork was complete and I was due in August which was a good thing. I told everyone, including my parents, that I was staying on in Edinburgh to take a class or two during the summer session but would be back in New York in time for the start of the fall semester at school. My finely-crafted plan in place, everything seemed under control.

But it wasn't. In July, when I was a full eight months along, I went into labor and gave birth to a little boy. He was still-born. I asked ... begged ... to see him. One of the nurses said that 'wasn't a good idea' but another, pitying me no doubt, appeared in the doorway carrying my lifeless baby in her arms. She brought him to the foot of my bed so I could see him. He was swaddled in a pale blue and white striped blanket. I never forgot his little face or that nurse's kindness.

I used the money I had saved tutoring and working at the tobacconist shop to bury my son in an Edinburgh cemetery. I named him Duncan, a good Scottish name. Physically, I bounced back quickly. I was glad to have some time to recover emotionally before I was expected home. I continued my tutoring work and also put in some hours at the tobacconist shop. The owners, Mr. and Mrs. Fraser, were so good to me. I suspected they knew my secret but they never said and never asked any questions. I was comfortable that I would have the money for my flight home, leaving as planned in August.

I went to the cemetery regularly in the weeks after Duncan's burial there. I brought small bouquets of fresh flowers and planned to eventually have a small marker put on his grave when I could afford it. One day as I stood looking down at his grave, I heard someone say my name. I looked up. It was Alec. I couldn't believe my eyes. He came forward and said he was surprised to see me at the cemetery. He said he had come to finalize arrangements for his grandmother's gravestone as she had passed away a month earlier. There was an awkward silence as he waited for me to say something. I offered my condolences for the loss of his grandmother and then the tears came and I began to sob pitifully. He ushered me up the walking path to a bench and sat down next to me. I turned toward him and looked up into his green eyes and then I told him about our son Duncan.

He was visibly shaken. I calmed myself and put my hand over his. I answered his questions and explained that I had never had any intention of disrupting his life and wedding plans and had arranged for the baby to be put up for adoption. He started to say he would have helped me if only I had told him. I asked that we not talk about the past and just remember Duncan . . . always. He offered to pay for any hospital bills or other expenses I might have. I told him that wasn't necessary. He asked if he could at least help pay for the burial costs. I thought for a moment and then said I planned to put a marker on Duncan's grave and he could help with the cost of that if he wanted to. We arranged to meet at Duncan's grave the following day and we did. I accepted the money he offered which was enough for the small marker I wanted for the grave.

Alec and Margaret were to be married the following week. I wished him well and said goodbye. He didn't ask for my contact information and I didn't ask for his. There was no point. Before I left for home, I ordered the grave marker. It would take several weeks to be made and installed. I told Mr. and Mrs. Fraser about Duncan. They each hugged me and comforted me with kind words. Their burrs were like a warm, soothing breeze caressing my ears. They asked me to take them to Duncan's grave as they planned to make visits there after I had gone home. They would always remember me and my *'wee bairn.'* When the grave marker was installed, they sent me a photograph of it.

The day before I left Edinburgh in August, I walked the Royal Mile from top to bottom for the last time. The streets were crowded with visitors who had come to see the famous Military Tattoo events at Edinburgh Castle and the performance theatrics of the Fringe arts festival. The air was alive with excitement and the sounds of music and merriment echoed along the way. Despite all that had happened, I loved and felt bound to that city as much as the first time I had wandered down those cobblestones.

When I saw my parents waving furiously to me at the airport, a rush of relief washed over me. My parents were elated to see me and so proud of their daughter, the international student. I would have dearly loved to tell them about Duncan but I never did. In fact, once home, I never told anyone until today, not even Sam.

Part Seven:

Caitriona

28. There's More Where That Came From

Secrets, damn them to hell I thought. They sap the life force out of us, casting shadows over our days, and haunting our dreams at night. We hold onto them the way hoarders hold onto their filthy, rancid possessions, fearing to lose control of them and so our lives. My thoughts flitted from Nora to Ellen to Nicola and I tallied up the enormous number of years that had been devoted to the maintenance of their secrets and at what cost to each of them.

In Nicola's case, she had paid a terrible price. The original secret, the fact that she had a college fling and a pregnancy that ended with the still-born birth of her baby son, was sad but not really shocking, especially in the days when the 'sexual revolution' was in full swing. Her decision not to tell her parents, friends, and others who knew her was no doubt the right thing but not telling Sam had ultimately fractured the foundation of their marriage.

Having gotten pregnant once (and so easily), Nicola assumed having children with Sam would not be a problem. She did get pregnant three times over the first five years of their marriage but miscarried all three times. After the third time, her doctor told her she should not try again because it would be too dangerous for her. Sam was not with her at that doctor visit and, perhaps because of that, the doctor asked somewhat nervously, if Nicola had only been pregnant the three times she miscarried. Her head, bowed in response to having been told she should not try again to have a baby, snapped up. She responded with a question: *Why would he ask her that?* His answer was that her uterus appeared to have scarring unrelated to her miscarriages.

Nicola never answered his question. She rose, thanked him for warning her about the risk of any additional pregnancies, and left the room. From that moment on, her original secret took on a new devastating element and its proportions grew. Her tryst with Alec Campbell was responsible for her being unable to have a baby with Sam. Over the years, the weight of her secret increased, fed by her guilt. She told herself that if she and Sam could have had children, he might not have become an alcoholic. Her deceit was at the heart of every problem in their marriage.

Nicola, unlike Ellen and me, was a planner, a plodder in fact. She moved forward in life with caution, perhaps because her impetuousness that night in Scotland altered her life. She made decisions slowly, with deliberate measured steps that brought her eventually to a conclusion. For Ellen and me, deliberateness took quite another form when it came to decision-making. It was a fluid, intuitive, and sometimes rapid process whereby we arrived at a decision, committing to it in short order. We did cannonballs into the pool, never testing the water before jumping in. Nicola, on the other hand, would stick her toes in first, dangle her ankles over the side for a bit, and then walk down the stairs into the pool. I understood the difficult journey she must have taken in preparation for telling me her secret and the emotional price she paid to do so. I hoped that, finally, she was free, her yoke thrown aside for good . . . but I wished she hadn't taken so long to decide it was time.

After hearing about Nicola's time in Scotland and her son Duncan, I was sure that I had to help her make the decision to go back to Edinburgh. I had wanted to do a few days in Scotland when Nicola and I made the trip to Ireland in search of my mother and father's origins and now it was a must. We would visit Duncan's grave together and then we would go to Ireland. No matter how it turned out, it was time to mend the frayed threads of our lives.

I amped up my genealogical research determined to find enough to justify the trip to Ireland. I contacted public and university libraries that had collections of books, documents, and newspapers related to Ireland in the decades between the achievement of Irish independence in 1921 and the mid-1950s when my mother Delia was sent to St. Gerard's. The internet made it possible to reach for resources almost anywhere. I set a goal of getting up-to-speed on what life in Ireland was like in the first few decades after Irish independence. I was aware of the 'Troubles,' the devastating armed conflict between republicans and loyalists in Northern Ireland, a tragedy that left both sides victim to violence from the late 1960s until the Good Friday Agreement in 1998.

According to Father Aloysius, my father was a republican activist with some group in the mid-1950s. I knew nothing about life in Ireland at that time and I didn't recall ever hearing about any IRA or other republican incidents in that era. My plan was to get a feel for the years when my mother and father would have been children and adolescents in Ireland and then focus in on the period when Delia became pregnant with me.

I worked methodically, tracking the sources I had used and mapping out a timeline. I found out that what genealogists say is true: chasing your family history is like assembling a complex, challenging jigsaw puzzle, putting together shards and fragments and leveraging those to reveal new clues. They also swear that when you think you have exhausted all avenues and couldn't possibly find anything else, you *will* find something new. That's just what happened to me. I followed my plan, educating myself about life in Ireland and then digging for information about the IRA and similar groups operating in the 1950s. There wasn't much republican activity to speak of and the scarcity of information at first seemed a bad thing, a potential dead-end. In fact, it turned out to be a good thing: less possibilities meant all I could do was comb through every bit and piece of the limited information that was available in the hope I would hit pay dirt.

My research revealed that between the late 1930s and early 1950s, the Irish Republican Army (IRA) had been significantly weakened as the result of aggressive government security measures in both the north and the south of the island. Membership in the IRA had waned due to arrests and internments and continued infighting between factions in the organization, some members vowing never to accept the partition of the island and believing that the governments in both the Republic of Ireland and Northern Ireland should be overthrown. By the early 1950s, IRA policy no longer supported armed action against the authorities of the Republic of Ireland. Instead IRA guerrilla operations would be organized in and launched from the Republic, their targets being in Northern Ireland.

Needing to rearm itself, the IRA first organized raids on British military facilities for that purpose. Once rearmed, plans were put in place for the new offensive in the North. Known as the Border Campaign or Operation Harvest, it began in December 1956 with the objective of driving the British out so that a united Ireland could be created. About two hundred IRA members were to fill the ranks of the guerilla units carrying out the campaign. That month there were bombings in Derry, Lisnaskea, and Enniskillen and burnings in Magherafelt and Newry, the most frequent targets being barracks of the RUC (Royal Ulster Constabulary). The campaign continued actively in 1957, eventually petering out a few years later and judged by most as a failure. One thing the Border Campaign did was to give the authorities in both Northern Ireland and the Republic of Ireland the justification needed to institute internment, meaning that on both sides of the border, hundreds of suspected IRA members were picked up and incarcerated without the right to a trial. Among those arrested and interned in the Republic in 1957 was eighteen-year-old Seamus Costello, a young IRA section leader whose exploits would provide a pivotal clue to my father's identity.

29. In League with the 'Boy General'

Seamus Costello, born into a middle-class family in County Wicklow in 1939, reportedly became a budding republican before the age of fifteen. By the young age of sixteen he had talked his way into IRA membership. Already understanding the role that politics would play in the quest for Irish unification, he joined Sinn Féin and became a political organizer as well. When the Border Campaign was put in motion Costello, then just seventeen, led an IRA unit active in the area of South Derry. His daring and success, including the burning of the Magherafelt Courthouse, earned him both the nickname 'Boy General' and support from some local Derry men who joined his unit. The fact that he operated in Derry and recruited there drew my interest since Father Aloysius had connected the Mother Superior at St. Gerard's to Derry.

After the incursions and operations in the Derry area, Seamus Costello and a few of his cohorts made it back to the Republic only to be arrested in 1957 and sentenced to six months at Mountjoy Prison in Dublin. At the time of their expected release, they were instead transferred to the Curragh prison camp in County Kildare as internees. One of the more challenging research avenues I pursued was locating Irish newspapers that reported on the Border Campaign. I tried searching the web with minimal results but I did find a few references to a publication titled *Irish Union* (in Irish: *Aontas Éireann*) reportedly aligned with Sinn Féin. The trick was to find copies of that long-shuttered newspaper so that I could read the actual articles.

That pursuit gave new meaning to the genealogy term 'brick wall.' I contacted libraries (state and university), the Library of Congress, historical societies and the like. I stopped counting how many inquiries I had made when the count reached over two dozen. When I was ready to pack it in, I circled back to contact two potential sources that had promised to get back to me but had not. One of those, an Irish historical society, told me they were sure they had emailed me to provide a promising source in Ireland. As it turned out, each of the two people looking into my request mistakenly thought the other had responded. After an apology I told them wasn't necessary, they gave me contact information for an archivist in Dublin and she emailed me the articles I was after.

Based on the short excerpt from one of the articles I had seen on the internet, I believed the full article would include the names of those arrested and interned for their participation in the Border Campaign. I was right and the list confirmed that a number of them were from Northern Ireland. I went through the list hoping to find a young man of eighteen or so whose home was listed as Derry or thereabouts. My eyes stopped at one name: Aiden O'Rinn from Strabane. (Strabane is near Derry, about twenty miles south.)

It took a minute for it to sink in. When Father Aloysius had given me the Mother Superior's name, I wrote it down as I heard it: *Sheila Orrin*. It was no doubt correctly spelled *O'Rinn* – it had to be. Could it be that my mother was not the one who was related to the Mother Superior but, instead, my father was? Wouldn't it be plausible that the O'Rinns were the ones who arranged for my mother to come to St. Gerard's, knowing that the child she was carrying was fathered by their son? My mind, on fire with possibilities and scenarios, hurtled ahead jumping to conclusions in rapid succession. More importantly, my intuitive senses told me I had it right. I just knew this was my breakthrough moment.

I took a few minutes to reground myself and then sketched out the next steps to be taken. Assuming my father was Aiden O'Rinn, he would have been interned the year after I was born. I had to find out everything I could about the Curragh prison camp and what became of the internees held there in the late 1950s. I shuttered at the thought that my father could have died or even been executed there.

Information about the Curragh camp was more readily available on-line due to its long history as a military facility and notoriety as an internment camp. The Boy General, Seamus Costello, was also the subject of a good deal of digital information owing to his life-long republican (and socialist) activism, a life that ended in 1977 when he was assassinated by a member of a rival republican group called the Official IRA. His politics, IRA ties, and his sensational death by gunshot in Dublin all contributed to Costello being remembered and documented. That meant I could grab his coattails for at least part of the journey to find my father, starting with their internment at Curragh.

First, I wanted to understand what 'the Curragh' was. Not the Curragh *prison camp* – the geographical place known as the Curragh. The Curragh is an area of about 5,000 acres of rolling grasslands, a plain formed in the aftermath of the last Ice Age. While the locale can trace its military connection back hundreds of years, the Curragh is now known as the hub of Irish thoroughbred racing. More intriguing are the age-old stories of the connection of St. Brigid, the patroness of Ireland, to the Curragh. One of the most often told stories is that Brigid came to Kildare hoping to find land on which a convent would be built. The land she selected belonged to the King of Leinster. When the King asked Brigid how much land she needed, she replied that she just wanted as much land as her cloak could cover. Intrigued by her answer, he agreed. She laid her cloak out on the ground and, as he watched, the cloak grew larger, spreading to cover all the acres now known as the Curragh plain.

It was quite a shifting of gears to change my focus from the image of the rolling Curragh grasslands back to the Curragh prison camp and Seamus Costello. Reports were that Costello used his time in the camp to hone his military skills, sharpen his political views, and learn more about other national struggles for independence. He was known to refer to his internment as his 'university days.'

Conditions at the camp were described as damp and dirty. Multiple sets of barbed wire fences surrounded the camp along with a booby-trapped trench. Armed guards were on patrol around the perimeter of the camp and in watch towers as well. Despite all that, escape attempts did occur, some successful. In December 1958, about a year-and-a-half after Seamus Costello and his men were interned, the largest escape happened when about two dozen men, some armed with wire cutters, charged the fences.

The guards were completely taken by surprise thus giving the escapees more time before bullets and ammonia grenades flew through the air. In the end, more than a dozen men got through the fences and just two were recaptured, the others hidden by local people. Seamus Costello was not one of the escapees. He and the remaining internees in the camp were released in the spring of

1959 when the Irish government ended its policy of internment without trial.

I couldn't find a list of the names of the prisoners who successfully escaped in December 1958 or a list of those released three months later but I hoped that, one way or the other, Aiden O'Rinn had gotten out and made his way back to Strabane. Convinced I was on the right trail and had enough leads to make the pilgrimage to Strabane, I began planning our trip to Ireland and Scotland.

30. Escape from New York

"Cat, I beg you, please stop humming that tune," Nicola said. "If I hear one more chorus of *Loch Lomond* I'm going to take a road, any road, out of here!"

"I was watching a PBS show about Scottish history last week and that song was part of the soundtrack," I said. "Ever since it's been looping in my head."

"Well," Nicola said, "since we are going to Scotland and that tune is all but an anthem over there, I should tell you about its origins. The music portion of the song was first published in 1841 in a volume titled *Vocal Melodies of Scotland*. There are multiple opinions about the origins of the lyrics, most related to the mid-18th century Jacobite rebels, who, led by Bonnie Prince Charlie, fought for the overthrow of the English king."

"Fought unsuccessfully," I said, "as I recall."

"Yes," Nicola said. "The high road is supposed to represent the road that takes the living back home while the low road carries the spirits of the dead home. In the end, all the Scots soldiers would come home, dead or alive."

"Another song inspired by the Gaelic struggle against the English," I replied. "I'll try to alternate between humming that and humming *Danny Boy* when we get over there."

"You're incorrigible," Nicola moaned.

Banter concluded, we went through the arrangements for our flights from New York to Edinburgh, Edinburgh to Belfast and Belfast to New York and our accommodations over the two weeks we would be in Scotland and Ireland. That mapped out, we worked on a daily itinerary of the specific places we needed to go. I could almost hear Nicola's breathing relax when she saw everything lined up and confirmed. The one thing I didn't tell her was that I had upgraded us to fly first class on the flights to and from Europe. That would be a surprise . . . and my treat.

We checked our passports (multiple times), pored over the TSA packing edicts, bought way too many boxes of small plastic bags to hold our liquids, and then there was the agonizing over what to pack. It was a good thing we started packing almost three weeks ahead because clothes and shoes went in and out over and over again until we faced up to the fact that each of us was over-packing and would have to maneuver that dead weight for fifteen days. We decided we would have a wash-day in either Edinburgh or Derry and would try the recommended monochromatic approach to packing: narrowing the number of colors so that tops and bottoms were easily interchangeable. That had the added benefit of reducing the urge to pack five pairs of shoes to coordinate with different outfits. I suggested that we *should* over-pack underwear (particularly 'drawers' as Nora would have called them), my rule being that you should never cut it close when it comes to having a clean pair at hand.

"Oh yes," Nicola smirked. "I know that's one of your rules to live by. When you fell on the ice and broke your kneecap, I had to rifle through your purse to find your insurance card and I happened upon a clean, spare pair of drawers in a Ziploc bag."

"You'll thank me Nic," I said returning the smirk, "if the haggis gets your pipes running."

"Oh man," Nicola grimaced. "Forget the haggis and, as for 'pipes,' I'll stick to the bagpipes, thank you very much. That reminds me, did we have Pepto and Kaopectate on the packing list?"

"Shit yes," I fired back.

As the day of our departure drew closer, I could see Nicola's anxiety ramping up even though she tried very hard to mask it. While the trip was something of an adventure for me, it was a reckoning for her. I was hoping for a discovery about my family and believed I was ready for that even if it wasn't a happy story, my biggest concern being that I would find nothing but another dead end. For Nicola, the trip was not about discovery. She knew what was waiting for her, a rush of memories that would become tangible again and reawakened feelings that could bring pain once more.

Soon enough we were at the airport for our evening flight and I coolly told Nicola that we were flying in first class. Her head snapped around in my direction and she grinned from ear-to-ear.

"No way!" she said.

"Oh yes, my friend," I said, "we're going to do this together and we're going to do it in style . . . our style, that is."

As we boarded, I heard her start humming *Loch Lomond* and I joined in.

31. Where the High and Low Roads Meet

The first thing that surprised me about Edinburgh was the size of the city. The trip from the airport by cab took at least a half-hour and we were treated to near-gridlock traffic and hair-raising lane changes as our cabbie navigated the way to Old Town Edinburgh. The second surprising thing was hearing myself use the word *enchanting* to describe the Royal Mile.

I had booked us into the Radcliffe House, a TripAdvisor favorite within walking distance of almost everything we wanted to see or do in Old Town. Aiming for convenience, great amenities and service, and immersion in the history of Edinburgh, I had selected the Radcliffe. A beautiful boutique hotel blending the classic historical details of an 1830s Georgian house with best elements of today's modern hotels, it also hosted an intriguing restaurant that served everything from Chateaubriand to Haggis Bonbons. The reviews on TripAdvisor were dead on. The Radcliffe did not disappoint.

Nicola hadn't said when she wanted to go to the cemetery to visit Duncan's grave. I wanted to give her as much support as possible but I was at a loss how to do that. Should I step back, not mentioning anything about the cemetery, giving her 'space?' Should I try to nudge her in the direction of making the visit right away – pulling off the Band-Aid in one quick tug? My dilemma was solved when Nicola told me she wanted to take me around to see the sights before we went to the cemetery. That seemed the kind of practical decision Nicola would make, a measured strategy. Toes in the water first, no cannonballs off the diving board.

On our first full day in the city, Nic locked arms with me and led me onto the cobblestone streets of old Edinburgh. I felt a bit like Dorothy when she stepped off on the yellow brick road – excited but unsure where we would wind up and what we might encounter along the way. We made the trek up the hill to Edinburgh Castle, snagged a pair of tickets, and continued the uphill walk into the enormous castle compound. She had told me that the interior castle road could easily handle the likes of a tractor-trailer and she wasn't exaggerating.

Nic made sure we hit all the highlights of the castle. I was very taken with the serenity of the little St. Margaret's Chapel built in the 12th century and still used for weddings and baptisms today and

I loved the dog cemetery where the remains of military dogs associated with army regiments have been laid to rest after their years of service. It goes without saying that the Crown Jewels of Scotland, including the priceless crown, scepter and sword used in the coronation of Mary, Queen of Scots in the 16th century, were amazing. In fact, 'Mary' herself, in the form of a well-acted in-character historical portrayal, made an appearance in the Great Hall of the castle and we thoroughly enjoyed her performance.

The theme of dogs and cemeteries continued later that day when we made our way to Greyfriars Kirkyard Cemetery, famous for the story of Bobby, the loyal terrier who mourned his deceased master there for more than a dozen years and was buried at the cemetery after his passing. A life-size statue of Bobby was put up in 1872 and is one of the top visitor sights in Edinburgh to this day.

Our first few days in Edinburgh flew by as we strolled up and down the Royal Mile, stopping for pub food and shopping along the way. We visited the imposing St. Giles Cathedral and eventually made it to the bottom of the road for a tour of Holyrood Palace, famous for its connection to Mary, Queen of Scots who was executed at the direction of her cousin, the first Queen Elizabeth.

We each bought a tartan kilt and loaded up on Scottish wool and cashmere accessories including scarves, hats, and gloves. Nic paused in front of one of the shops and told me it was the location that had housed the tobacconist shop where she had worked and had met Alec Campbell. When we got back to the hotel, she said we would visit Duncan's grave the next day.

In the morning, we ate breakfast at the hotel and asked that a cab be called to pick us up and take us to the cemetery since it was not quite in walking distance. We bought some fresh flowers across the street from the cemetery office and then went in to confirm the location of Duncan's grave. After over forty years, the cemetery population had grown and Nic wasn't sure of her bearings.

Nic and I approached the receptionist who looked up and asked if she could be of assistance. Nicola explained that we were from the States and had come to visit her son Duncan's grave after many years and needed help to find the plot. The receptionist asked for Duncan's full name and date of death or burial. After getting that information she went to one of the imposing wood bookcases and pulled out a volume, leafing through it. She followed her finger down the pages until she found the entry for Duncan. She wrote down the location information and provided a map, marking the actual gravesite. Nicola thanked her softly, put her sunglasses back on, and we left the office.

I looped my arm through Nic's this time, sure she needed support. It was a beautiful sunny day with a crisp autumn breeze that put a bit of a chill in the air. We walked shoulder-to-shoulder and I almost felt we were reliving Duncan's funeral day as we slowly walked the winding path. It took almost ten minutes to get to Duncan's grave and as we approached it, I heard Nicola sniffing and felt her shoulders rising as the tears came.

There was a cast iron bench right near the grave and we sat down there to catch our breath. The grave had a small black granite monument engraved with the baby's full name, Duncan Dunn, and a symbol called an eternity knot that represented the continuum of existence - no beginning and no end. Nicola stood and walked close to the grave shaking her head as if confused. She turned to me and pointed to some small engraved lettering under Duncan's name. I crouched down to get a better look. It said *'Wee Bairn, Never Forgotten.'* She pulled a dog-eared photo out of her pocket and handed it to me.

"That engraving under Duncan's name was not ordered by me and it wasn't there when the stone was installed," Nicola said, almost sounding a little panicky. "The Frasers sent me the photo you're holding. It was taken shortly after the monument was set. You can see that those four words are not on the gravestone."

"Could the Frasers have added those words themselves, after the fact?" I asked. "You told me they said Duncan would never be forgotten."

"I can't believe they would have done that without asking me," Nicola said. "They were not the kind of people to take such a liberty. No, no, they wouldn't. We have to go back to the office and have them check their records about how this happened."

We made the long walk back to the cemetery office only to find it had closed for the day. I saw the look of anguish on Nicola's face. She was shaken by the realization that Duncan's gravestone had been altered. I told her we would come back the following morning to get to the bottom of things. The rest of the day and evening found us both subdued. We picked at our food, drank a bit too much, and hit the sack, alarm set to ensure an early start the following morning.

32. Grave Revelations

There wasn't much sleeping that night for either of us. I tossed and turned and heard Nic get up several times. The morning couldn't come soon enough for either of us. When it did, we showered, dressed, and were in the dining room just as they were opening for breakfast. Uninterested in perusing the menus, we just ordered the standard Scottish breakfast and, after eating very little the evening before, did our best to clean our plates and fortify ourselves for what would no doubt be another stressful day.

The cab dropped us near the cemetery office about fifteen minutes before it opened. We paced back and forth on the walkway until we saw the receptionist unlocking the door. We pretty much followed her inside and planted ourselves in front of her desk as she got settled.

"Ladies," she said a bit curtly, "back so soon?"

That was all Nicola needed to hear. Gloves were off and she leaned over the front of the desk and began the interrogation after first looking down to check out the name plate on the desk top.

"Ms. Murray," she said. "When I visited my son's grave yesterday I noticed something peculiar with respect to his gravestone. There is engraving that was not part of the original monument order I had authorized at the time of my son's death."

Ms. Murray, not yet sensing the direction of things, made no response but for a blank look that conveyed no appreciation of the agitation of the woman hovering over her. Nicola pulled the old photo of the grave monument out of her pocket and extended it to Ms. Murray. Then she took out her phone and pulled up a photo of the monument taken the prior day and clearly showing the additional 'unauthorized' engraving.

"Well," Nicola said, "do you see what I mean? I never gave permission for the monument to be altered in any way. I want to know when that additional engraving was added and by whom. Kindly check your records right now and give me that information."

"I will need to see some identification before giving you any information," Ms. Murray said as she rose from her chair so she was eye level with Nicola. "These records are confidential as I am sure you understand."

I saw the red rising in Nicola's cheeks and stepped in. "Nic, show her the carbon copy of the plot deed you showed me yesterday and your passport. That should be all the proof needed."

Nicola opened her tote and produced the copy of the deed and her passport. Ms. Murray looked both over, returned the passport, and asked if she could make a photocopy of the deed. Nicola said yes. Once the copy was made, Ms. Murray asked us to take a seat while she located the grave file.

"Jesus," Nicola said. "I hope this place has computerized their records or we will be here for God knows how long."

Most of the records were computerized. Ms. Murray returned in about ten minutes, file in hand. She explained that the additional engraving was done about twelve years earlier.

"On what authority?" Nicola asked.

"At the request of Mr. Alec Campbell, the father of the deceased," Ms. Murray replied, looking sheepish.

Left momentarily speechless, Nic and I turned to each other as if to confirm we had both heard the same thing. Then Nic, eyes narrowed, fired the next round. "Well," she said, "since you are so strict about getting proper identification, how did a man named Campbell convince you that he was Duncan Dunn's father?"

"I was not working here at that time," Ms. Murray said, "but the file contains a copy of the original grave deed and an affidavit from Mr. Campbell attesting to his paternity. There was an attempt to call a Mr. and Mrs. Fraser who were listed as the local contacts in the grave file but they apparently had died years earlier. On the basis of Mr. Campbell's affidavit and his possession of the original deed, the engraving work was done as he requested. It was completed at the same time that engraving was also added to the monument on the other grave owned by Mr. Campbell."

Nicola's mouth worked and her head moved from left to right and back again in disbelief. When she didn't speak, I took over the interrogation asking Ms. Murray the obvious question: what 'other grave owned by Mr. Campbell?'

Ms. Murray, realizing she had said too much, reluctantly gave us the location of the second grave but nothing more. With that, Nicola and I exited the office and regrouped outside. As we walked toward the location of the Campbell gravesite, Nicola tried to reason out how Alec Campbell got the deed to Duncan's plot. She had left that document with the Frasers so that they could act as her representative if needed, keeping the carbon copy herself.

We found the Campbell grave which was almost back-to-back with Duncan's and silently read the inscriptions:

Maisie Blaire Campbell   1979 – 1996

Margaret Kelsey Campbell 1946 - 2004

There was room for a third name on the grave monument and both of us felt sure that was reserved for Alec Campbell. We knew the woman he was to marry was named Margaret and we concluded that Maisie was their daughter, lost to death at the tender age of sixteen or seventeen. Things were getting complicated.

We made our way out of the cemetery and as we passed the office I made an excuse to go inside, telling Nicola I needed to ask to use the bathroom. Nicola smirked and said she wished me luck considering our earlier tangle with Ms. Murray. I went inside. Ms. Murray looked up and let out a long breath. I turned on my best schmooze, told her the sad story of Duncan's birth (short version) and asked if she might have contact information for Alec Campbell. Appealing to her heartstrings, I pleaded, saying that this would be the last chance for Duncan's parents, who still mourned the baby they had lost, to reconcile their shared past. She opened the file, still on top of her desk, and scribbled down a phone number without saying a word. Then I pushed the envelope all the way and asked to use the bathroom.

"Well," said Nicola, when I rejoined her on the sidewalk, "did she let you breach the bathroom or will we have to wander down the street looking for a pub so you can relieve yourself?"

"Ms. Murray had mercy on me but let's still find a pub. I could use a drink and you must need one too Nic."

33. For Auld Lang Syne

"You had no right," Nicola howled. "How could you put me in this position?"

"How could you leave here without trying to contact him, setting yourself up for more regrets later?" I said. "There was no way we could have foreseen all this or planned for it. Sometimes you just have to jump in and take a risk. This is absolutely one of those times."

"You weren't thinking about me," Nicola snarled. "When you saw that his daughter died at about the same age as your Gemma, you identified your loss with his as if you two were some kind of kindred spirits."

She must have seen that those words struck me like a spray of bullets and instantly regretted them. I wanted to say how unfair her accusation was but somewhere in the recesses of my mind I began to question my motives in contacting Alec Campbell. Before I could respond, she spoke again.

"Oh Cat, please forgive me, please forgive me," she pleaded through a rush of tears. "I didn't mean that. I swear I didn't. I lashed out at you because I feel a complete loss of control over what's happening to me. Instead of this visit bringing me closure, it has upended everything, including my carefully orchestrated plan for how I would handle returning to Edinburgh. Please, please forgive me."

"There's nothing to forgive," I said. "I have been twisting your arm to get you here since you told me about Duncan, assuming that what I would do in your situation is what you should do. I think I should be the one doing the apologizing. I can call him and cancel the meeting if you want me to."

"I don't know what I want at this point," Nicola said. "How can a sixty-five-year-old woman be afraid to meet a seventy-year-old man? It's almost laughable. Tell me again what you said to him and how he responded."

"I called the number Ms. Murray gave me and asked for Alec Campbell. The man who answered said he was Alec Campbell and asked who was calling. I took a deep breath and started by giving my name and saying I was from the States and visiting Edinburgh with a friend he might know. I think that was enough for him to leap ahead and conclude that my 'friend' was you . . . but he didn't say. I decided to just cut to the chase and told him I was traveling with you and that we had visited Duncan's grave and saw the new engraving on the stone and found out he had ordered it. I told him that coming back and going to the grave had been very hard for you and that seeing the extra engraving and finding out how it got there had been a shock. I confessed that I had been the one who encouraged, almost pressured, you to return to Edinburgh and I was very concerned you would leave without the closure you were seeking. I finished by saying I thought that it might be good for both of you to have a chance to meet and reconcile your mutual past. Then I asked if he would be willing to do that. He hardly paused before saying 'yes' and he recommended you meet at the bench near Duncan's grave tomorrow morning at eleven. If you want me to cancel, I will phone him and call it off right now."

"I can't do that to him," Nicola said. "I would feel like we were toying with him . . . with his emotions . . . especially now that I know he was faithful to Duncan's memory all these years. Since this is your doing, you'll have to go with me and broker the reunion just in case things don't go well."

"Alright then," I said. "I guess we know what we're doing on our last full day in Edinburgh."

In what felt very much like the movie *Groundhog Day*, morning came, we picked at our breakfasts, and took a cab to the cemetery.

As we approached Duncan's grave, we saw a man sitting on the bench, his back to us. I squeezed Nicola's hand as we walked toward him. Probably hearing our footsteps, he rose and turned in our direction. He was tall, medium build, with a full head of gray hair still streaked with its original deep brown color. I suspected that his arresting greens eyes were just as Nicola remembered them.

"Hello," he said, smiling slightly.

"Hello Alec," said Nicola. "This is my friend Cat . . . Caitríona. You spoke with her on the phone."

I walked forward and extended my hand. "Yes, Alec, I'm the brassy Yank who called you. It's very nice to meet you."

Alec motioned to Nicola to sit down on the bench. She hesitated, looking at me. I nodded in the direction of the bench and then told her that I was headed out to a museum about two blocks away.

"I'm going to soak up a bit of local culture," I said. "Take as much time as you need. If I tire of improving myself, I'll do a little shopping. Call me when you want to meet up."

I made a quick turn and moved away, not waiting for Nic to respond. As I was passing the cemetery office, I made a snap decision to stop in to see Ms. Murray for the last time. The look on her face when I came through the door was priceless, a crazy quilt of expressions that communicated how much she wished it wasn't me standing in front of her desk again.

"Ms. Murray," I said with a smile. "My friend Nicola and Mr. Campbell are right now sitting together near their baby son's grave, speaking about him and their shared past for the first time in over forty-five years. I just stopped in to thank you most sincerely for your part in making this happen."

"It's kind of you to give me some of the credit for their reconciliation," Ms. Murray said, "but this is not at all my doing and, truth be told, it is not even you that made it happen, although you may understandably think so. This is wee Duncan's work and now that it is done, he can rest in peace. I have worked here long enough to have seen the effects of the spiritual energy of the community of souls resident in this place . . . and so it is with this."

Having nothing meaningful to say in response, I just nodded and left the office, heading for the museum. About ninety minutes later, my phone rang. It was Nic. She asked me to meet her . . . and Alec . . . at the pub up the street for a bite of lunch. I felt my shoulders relax with relief. It must have gone well if he was joining us for lunch. As I walked back to the pub, I found myself humming the tune to *Auld Lang Syne*, that Scottish title loosely, and in this case fittingly, translating to *days gone by*.

Part Eight:

Nicola

34. High-Flying

"Cat, not now," I said impatiently. "I will tell you everything, every last detail. Let's just get through the check-in gauntlet and to the gate. I can't relax until I know we will be on the flight to Belfast."

Caitríona had a streak of relentlessness that, once triggered, was laser-focused. After our meeting and lunch with Alec, I was spent. When we got back to the Radcliffe, we were supposed to pack to get ready for our flight to Ireland but I had stretched out on the sofa to rest my eyes and promptly fell asleep for a good two hours. Cat, giving up on getting anything out of me at that point, started packing. When I woke up, a little dazed and disoriented, I pitched in and then we went for dinner. I gave Cat the basic recounting of my time on the bench with Alec, promising more details to come, and answered her most urgent questions. Yes, we exchanged postal and email addresses and phone numbers. Yes, we plan to keep in touch. No, he did not kiss me . . . nor did I jump him this time. Yes, his green eyes were still amazing . . . very. No, he never told his wife about Duncan or me.

We made it to the gate for the EasyJet flight from Edinburgh to Belfast and relief washed over me. This would be short hop flight, nothing like the long, pampered flight in first class from New York to Edinburgh. Cat elbowed me and flicked her head in the direction of a group of chattering young girls. There were eight of them, about eighteen to twenty years old, decked out in plastic tiaras, garish hot pink feather boas, and way too much rhinestone jewelry. As we gawked at them, a gentleman sitting on the other side of me leaned in and, in a pleasing Scots burr, explained that the group was 'a hen party out for some weekend fun.'

Cat and I, the hens and the rest of the passengers boarded and in about an hour we landed in Belfast. Although this leg of our adventure belonged to Cat, I had inserted myself in the planning of our movements and itinerary. I was well aware of her tendency for 'cannonball' entrances but was able to convince her to proceed in a more measured way that would let us see some of the countryside and sights on the way to Strabane. We picked up a rental car at the airport and headed for the Titanic Belfast museum. Cat and I had both seen and loved the movie so the chance to see the much-praised museum was irresistible.

The museum, situated on the small island where the Titanic was built by Harland & Wolff, is a juxtaposition of modern design and historic recreation. The striking architecture of the museum's massive jutting textured aluminum facade, on scale with Titanic's bow, is just as often interpreted as representative of the iceberg that took the ship down. Inside, in over a 100,000 square feet of amazing exhibit space, history comes alive in recreations of the days when Titanic was built and Belfast was a hub of the shipbuilding industry. All in all, the museum is the very definition of an *experience*. Need I say we were so very glad we didn't miss it?

Leaving Belfast, we drove north up the coast road. I did most of the driving since I was sure Cat's heavy foot and driving 'backwards' were not a good mix. I had made reservations at a B&B not far from the Giants Causeway and a few other must-see sights. The B&B was a lovely old country house eclectically decorated in a combination of antique furnishings and recent Asian tchotchkes. Our host was equally unique, both innkeeper and unsolicited tour guide authoritatively instructing his guests what to see and when to see it for the best possible experience. While his methods drew eye rolls from some of his guests, we had to admit he was spot-on with his recommendations.

We hit the rope bridge at Carrick-a-Rede. Well, I did anyway, fear of heights being one of Cat's few Achilles heels, not to mention that the climb down to the rope bridge on a metal ladder was no place for Cat's bum knee. She did watch me amble across and back and took some photos. Next we drove to the Giants Causeway, a place that challenged Cat's fear of heights in style. Summoning her courage and with help from me and another visitor, she scaled the strange cylinder-shaped stones. The look of triumph mixed with terror on her face was classic.

"Did you see that TV ad with Rick Steves where he visits here with a local who explains the legend of Finn McCool and these crazy stones?" I asked.

"Yep, I've seen it," Cat said. "How the hell am I going to get down from here in one piece?"

"Maybe you won't," I laughed. "Only kidding, we'll get you down, even if we have to call for a helicopter."

We did make it down and then walked the shoreline and up the path onto the overlooking cliffs. Words can't adequately describe the panoramic views or the feeling of being near or atop the stones. Mercifully for Cat, our next stop didn't involve taking on fear-inducing heights. Dunluce Castle (well, its remains) is a fortification on a rocky outcrop over the sea, its towers dating to the 14th century although there was likely some form of defenses there hundreds of years earlier. It is hauntingly engaging, awash in imaginings of romantic days of old, and is prime picture-taking territory. (I thank God for digital cameras as there was no end of picture-perfect scenes in dear Erin.)

We lunched in nearby Portrush and took the tour of the Bushmills Distillery. I choked on the free sample of Irish whiskey offered at the end of the tour, being no drinker of the hard stuff. Cat downed it like a pro. After the fire in my throat cooled, we were off to Derry and about to get down to the search for Cat's parents, Delia Doherty and (theoretically) Aiden O'Rinn, IRA fighter.

We got to Derry mid-morning, dropped our bags off at the B&B in the Cityside section, left the car there and set off for a tour of the historic city walls. It was a slow day for tourists due to off and on rain and we wound up getting our own private tour led by a local who supplemented his income as an actor with gigs as a guide. He was middle-aged, a bit chubby, and with the flare and animation you might expect from a performer. He took us on an entertaining and informative ramble explaining that Derry, situated on the west bank of the River Foyle, is the only remaining completely intact walled city in Ireland, boasting twenty-four original cannons, and rivaling the best examples of European walled cities. When the walk around the walls was completed, I expected our guide to leave us but, instead, he offered to walk us down to the area known as Bogside or 'Free Derry,' the Catholic stronghold neighborhood. Since we had every intention of making our way there anyway, we accepted his offer and went with him.

His jovial narrative became more subdued as we walked down the hill toward the Bogside neighborhood. As we got closer, I recognized the enormous two-story political murals painted on the sides of residential buildings. I had seen and read about them online and although I didn't need our guide to explain their political purpose or symbolism, I just listened to him describe their origins and the people who were pictured in the paintings. His personal connection to their significance was clear. Still, neither Cat nor I were prepared for his emotional explanation of the Bloody Sunday Memorial, erected in memory of fourteen locals gunned down by British troops during a peaceful demonstration in 1972. It had taken thirty-eight years for the British government to finally admit that those deaths were unjustified murder and for the names of the unarmed innocent dead, once characterized as armed IRA terrorists, to have their good names restored. I had a lump in my throat just hearing about it and could not imagine how powerfully the Bloody Sunday events and aftermath were felt by Derry Catholics.

When he left us, we wandered around ourselves and then made our way back to the B&B in almost complete silence. It was obvious to me that Cat had been very moved by what she had seen and heard and I could almost see the wheels turning in her brain as she contemplated the Irish Catholic nationalist heritage that was quickly becoming a linchpin of who she was and where she came from.

35. The Tell-All

The few days of leisurely driving along the coast provided the perfect opportunity for me to keep my promise to tell Cat all about my talk with Alec. It came in fits and starts punctuated by questions she could not wait to ask. It's a wonder I didn't drive off the side of one of the narrow winding roads as she repeatedly derailed the continuity of my story with one interruption after another.

When Cat had made her escape from the cemetery leaving Alec and me alone, the first few minutes were fraught. Awkwardness and anxiety kept us silent as we both looked down at the ground, hands folded in our laps. Since it was our doing that he was there, I decided I should suck it up and start the conversation.

"I understand you arranged for the added engraving on Duncan's gravestone," I said, still looking down. "How did you get the original grave deed that you submitted to get authorization from the cemetery for that work?"

I sensed the movement of his head in my direction as he replied. "I got it from Mr. Fraser years ago. When his wife passed away and his health worsened, he gave me the deed. I had first encountered the Frasers at the cemetery just a few years after you left for home. At first, just polite nods were exchanged. I wasn't ready to tell anyone I was Duncan's father. At some point, after running into me there multiple times, the Frasers, being polite, introduced themselves and I reciprocated. When I saw no obvious sign of recognition on their part, I assumed they did not know Duncan's father's name. On some instinct or whim, I purchased the grave behind Duncan's and also paid for a bench to be put in near his grave. It was what you Americans call a 'don't ask, don't tell' situation. I was sure they knew I was Duncan's father but they didn't ask and I didn't tell."

I finally got the courage to turn my face in his direction. I felt the ice break and the imaginary gap between us close. I bit down on my lower lip as it quivered. He saw it and patted my hand. Then I asked the harder question.

"Did you ever tell your wife about Duncan?" I asked.

"No," he said. " I deceived her throughout our marriage. Did you tell your husband?"

"No," I said. "I hid it from him, from my parents, from everyone in my life, until I told Cat just recently. How did you know I was married?"

"After Margaret died and I was alone and feeling so many regrets, I looked for you on-line, did a search for your name. Since I didn't know your married name, I didn't get very far until a photo came up with a caption that listed you as Nicola Dunn with your husband Sam Salvati. Once I saw you were married, I didn't try to find your contact information."

"I remember that photo," I said smiling. "It was taken at a cancer research fundraiser. Sam died a couple years later . . . cancer."

That exchange of honesty was healing for both of us. Our conversation was fluid thereafter, even the hard parts. Alec told me that Margaret had not wanted children but, after her unplanned pregnancy and the birth of Maisie, she was ecstatic, a doting mother. Maisie was the joy and center of their lives, a smart, impish little girl full of curiosity and questions. Everything changed when she was fourteen and was diagnosed with leukemia. At the start, treatment seemed successful. Those positive results and Maisie's infectious optimism about the future ruled the day . . . until the remission ended and the prognosis was dire. When Maisie died, Margaret was inconsolable. She withdrew from everyone including Alec and lost all interest in living. The next six years were a jumble of depression, doctors, and general desperation as to Margaret's condition. Alec had no time to grieve, that being both a good and a bad thing. He came home from the university one afternoon and found Margaret in bed. She looked more peaceful than he had seen her in years. As he approached the bed he realized something was wrong. She was gone, the official cause of death being recorded as a heart attack. Although there was no note, no narcotics or empty pill bottles, Alec couldn't help wondering if she had ended her life. He prayed that whatever the cause of her death, Margaret was reunited with Maisie.

In that ninety-minute conversation in the cemetery I got to know Alec Campbell and he, me. In truth, other than sharing a lost baby boy, we had had no other meaningful connection or knowledge of each other. As we sat on the bench, I told him about my background, my family and childhood, and about my life after I lost Duncan and left Edinburgh. He did the same. There was much more tragedy than triumph in those stories but the sharing created a bond between us beyond Duncan. I was sure we would keep in touch and even hoped we might see each other again one day.

After telling it all to Cat and weathering the barrage of her questions, I felt my equilibrium restored and a sense of completion. Now all we had to do was survive our quest to reconnect Cat to her Irish family roots. How hard could that be after what we pulled off in Scotland?

36. Home to Tyrone

It was time to move on to Strabane. I had booked reservations at a lovely rectory converted to a B&B. (What would we do without TripAdvisor?) It was actually just over the border near Lifford in County Donegal. It was the nicest of all the places we had stayed, large rooms with a sitting area, lots of antiques, a library with a fireplace, and fantastic hosts, Maeve and Dennis, who couldn't do enough for us. I was glad to spend our last several days in such a perfect place.

While making pleasant small-talk with our hosts, I explained what had brought us to the area. They were intrigued. Maeve said she had a childhood friend named Eileen living in Strabane for many years and offered to put us in touch with her if we liked. We asked how long the woman had lived in Strabane. Maeve said it had been at least twenty-five years. She had been widowed at a young age and returned to Strabane to help her mother care for her grandmother. By the time the grandmother passed away at a ripe old age, Eileen's mother's health was failing. Eileen cared for her mother and just stayed on after her mother's death.

"Eileen has a special gift of compassion for the elderly," Maeve said with obvious admiration. "They are drawn to her and she has a way of reaching and comforting them. She is forever opening her front door to find the old folks of Strabane and its surrounds seeking her care and counsel and she never turns them away. The local doctor and his nurse rely on her to alert them when someone needs medical attention. She does a great service for her community and expects nothing in return."

"We're looking for people from the area with the surnames Doherty and O'Rinn," Cat said. "Do you know any families with those names or would you have a phone directory we could check for them?"

"I don't know anyone with those names," Maeve said. "I'll need to call Eileen to see if she has the Strabane area directory. It's just a short way across the bridge from Lifford to Strabane but, mind you, it's a different country," she said wryly.

We had to laugh at the way she schooled us on that point and were very grateful for her willingness to help us. She soon called Eileen and we were invited to come see her that afternoon. Maeve baked some delicious brown bread and brought that with her when she joined us for the outing to meet Eileen. I was beginning to understand why Americans who visited Ireland raved about the generosity and hospitality of the Irish.

Eileen was a petite woman with finely-lined porcelain skin and light-colored hair with undertones of what once must have been a much bolder copper shade. Her modest but immaculate cottage was very welcoming, like its owner. She served us tea and Maeve's brown bread that we slathered with fresh Irish butter. It was heaven. After tea, Eileen brought us the local directory. We found two listings for Dohertys in Strabane and one listing for O'Rinn in nearby Castlederg. We took down the numbers and addresses and Cat said she would phone each of them that evening.

"Oh no darlin'," Maeve said, "that won't work. Let me or Eileen make the inquiries. Getting a strange call from an American asking questions about family members will get you nowhere. Do understand where you are and what has happened in the past. People in the North have a lot more secrets and painful family memories going back to the Troubles and even before. None of it has truly been forgotten."

Thank God for the karma or serendipity that brought us to stay with Maeve. As much as we had read about the IRA, particularly in the days when Cat's father would have been a member, we couldn't expect to understand the multigenerational effects of decades of social unrest and senseless violence. An image of the memorial monument in Derry for the Bloody Sunday victims came back to me and I recalled our tour guide's emotional explanation of its significance. Cat and I would be asking local people to trust us and share very personal stories about their family history. Maeve was dead-on. We would need to rely on her and Eileen to make the overtures and build some trust with the people who would be the key to confirming Cat's roots.

The calls were made as promised but without any real success. The number for one of the Dohertys was no longer in service and the other Doherty family was unwilling to talk about their family. A young girl answered the phone at the number listed for the O'Rinn family and took a message asking her father to call Eileen.

The following morning Eileen called. She had heard back from Michael O'Rinn, the man from Castlederg, and had set up a meeting for that afternoon at four o'clock at a pub not far from his home. Cat was ecstatic. We drove to Eileen's an hour or so earlier so we could walk through Cat's family story (what Cat knew and what she surmised) and give Eileen a chance to get familiar with the details and ask any questions she had. I knocked on Eileen's front door. She opened it, gave us a bright smile, and we followed her inside to find two elderly ladies having a cup of tea at the kitchen table.

"Caitríona and Nicola," Eileen said, turning from us toward the two ladies, "I'd like you to meet my friends, Miss Mary Higgins and her twin sister Miss Anna Higgins. Come sit down with us for a bit before we leave to Castlederg."

Mary and Anna Higgins appeared to be in their mid-seventies. They looked quite alike but Mary was heavier than Anna and I saw a cane propped up against her chair. It was quickly evident that Mary had the stronger personality of the two, if not the more robust physical presence. I tried not to be obvious as I kept checking my watch not wanting to be even a minute late for the meeting with Michael O'Rinn.

Eileen brought a cup of tea for me and another for Cat and sat down at the table. She took a sip of her tea and began telling us how Miss Mary had phoned her the day before asking that she stop by to see Miss Anna who had a cough and refused to see the doctor. When she visited their home she mentioned her new American friend who had come to Strabane in search of her Irish roots, specifically her parents. The Higgins sisters, always interested in getting a local scoop ahead of their neighbors, asked Eileen what family names were being looked into. Eileen, not wanting to betray Cat's confidence by revealing too much of the story of her birth, simply said the mother's family name was Doherty and the father's was O'Rinn. Eileen went on to tell them that calls had been made to two Doherty families in Strabane with no luck but that a promising contact had been made with an O'Rinn family in Castlederg.

"That's when we told her!" said Mary excitedly. "Our own mother, her name was Orla McDaid, had an older sister Fiona who married a man named Willie Doherty here in Strabane. Imagine! We may be your family, my dear. Anna and I are going to call our Uncle McDaid in Derry. He was the youngest of the McDaid children and is the last one living. He's all of ninety-one but still lives on his own and his memories of the old days are quite good. We'll get to the bottom of it just like Inspector George Gently."

"Oh Mary," laughed Anna, "Inspector Gently indeed!"

Eileen explained that Mary was referring to a character on a television show. They were amazed when we told them we were also fans of the dashing gray-haired police inspector and watched the show at home. Mary and Anna promised to call their uncle that evening. We gave them a lift home and then left for Castlederg.

37. May the Road Rise Up to Meet You

We pulled up to the pub in Castlederg with about two minutes to spare. We walked in and looked around. There were a few people at the bar but no one approached us. Eileen asked the man behind the bar if he knew Michael O'Rinn. He did. We ordered three coffees and, before taking them to a table in the corner, asked the bartender to motion to us when Mr. O'Rinn came in. Five minutes went by, then ten, and I saw the strain and disappointment on Cat's face. There's a risk in getting your hopes up.

At thirteen minutes after four, the pub door opened and we heard the bartender call out: "Mick O'Rinn, how are ya keeping?"

"Well enough Brian," the man answered with a broad smile. "Better when you pour me a Guinness."

Eileen got up, approached Mick O'Rinn, introduced herself, and brought him over. We stood, shook his hand, and Cat explained that she was the one in search of her parents who she believed were from the Strabane area. She told him she had recently found out she was adopted and was the daughter of a teenage girl named Delia Doherty who became pregnant and was sent from Ireland to an unwed mothers home in New York. Delia had later returned home to Ireland, leaving her newborn baby daughter in New York temporarily, promising to come back for her.

"So, you are the baby girl she left behind in New York then?" he asked.

"Yes," Cat said, "and when Delia never came back for me, I was raised by the two women who had temporary custody of me. I was told that one of them was my mother and the other my aunt. After they were both dead, our family priest gave me a letter from the woman I thought was my aunt. It said I was adopted. I've been digging for the truth since then, turning over every stone in the hope of finding out who I really am. My research has convinced me my father was a young man named Aiden O'Rinn. He was born in the late 1930s and became involved with the IRA in the 1950s during their Border Campaign. I found some old newspaper articles about the IRA raids that took place in this area, including the burning of a courthouse in Magherafelt, reportedly carried out under a young IRA section commander named Seamus Costello."

Before Cat could continue, Mick stood up and waved to an older man who had just entered the pub and said it was his father Rory

O'Rinn. Mick had told his father about Eileen's phone call and the planned meeting. Rory, no doubt a bit wary of an American out to prove a family connection, told Mick he would join him for the meeting. Mick pulled up another chair for his father and introductions were made once again. Mick caught his father up on the story Cat had told him thus far. When he got to the part about the Border Campaign and Seamus Costello, I saw a change in Rory's facial expression. He had been listening with something of a poker face up to that point – his reactions controlled and unreadable. It seemed that hearing the name Seamus Costello changed that, and quickly. His eyes widened and his eyebrows lifted. He deflected by taking a good gulp of his beer as he tried to regain his previous composure.

"Dad, do you know about this man Costello or a relation named Aiden O'Rinn?" Mick said, no doubt having noticed his father's reaction to the name.

"I know of Costello, but what has he got to do with you Miss?" he said, looking straight at Cat. "He came up this way for the IRA but he wasn't from here. He was from the Republic."

"When he was up here for the IRA raids, Costello recruited young men from this area for his IRA unit," Cat said. "One of them was named Aiden O'Rinn. It's Aiden O'Rinn that I believe may have been my father."

"And just why did you settle on Aiden O'Rinn as the man who was your father?" Rory asked Cat pointedly.

Cat backtracked to explain that it appeared her mother Delia was sent to St. Gerard's in New York because that facility was managed by a relation, a nun from the Derry area named Sheila O'Rinn. Hearing that name had an immediate effect on Rory O'Rinn, no doubt about that. His pursed lipped silence had all of us waiting in suspense.

"Sheila O'Rinn, God rest her soul," Rory said, "was my own aunt. She left home for America for the religious life before I was born. The family was most proud of her. I cannot say the same for Aiden O'Rinn."

"So Dad," Mick said, "you've heard of this Aiden O'Rinn. Is he related to us then?"

"Get me another beer Mick," said Rory. "I'll be needing it and whilst you're at it, order some food for the five of us as this is going to take some time."

38. My Brother's Keeper

Mick came back with a beer for his father and said he ordered some food. Rory drained the last of his first beer and took a swallow of the new one. Cat and I were trying our best to be patient and calm even though we both wanted to yell *let's get on with it*. Finally, Rory put down his beer and began.

"Aiden O'Rinn was my cousin. He was about ten years older than me. His father Patrick and my father Michael were brothers. Their sister was Sheila who became Sister Mary Brigid and went to America."

"So Mother Superior's name was Sister Mary Brigid," Cat blurted out, turning to me.

Rory went on. "Patrick was just a young boy when the Easter Rising happened. My father and Sheila were born a few years after that. My grandmother O'Rinn had other pregnancies but lost all those babies early on leaving only those three. Young Patrick was all of twelve or thirteen when independence came to the southern counties and the civil war broke out and it made an impression that stayed with him. My father told me Patrick was always asking the old-timers to tell him stories about the IRB . . . the Irish Republican Brotherhood I mean . . . and read every book about the fight for independence and the republicans he could find. He believed that all of Ireland must be reunited and free of the British. That never changed."

"Do you know if he shared those stories and beliefs with his son Aiden?" Cat asked, already guessing what was coming next.

"So my father told me," Rory replied. "Aiden first heard those stories sitting on his father's knee. The republicans were heroes fighting for the Irish people, and for equality and freedom for Catholics."

"So Granda Michael felt differently than his brother Patrick?" Mick asked.

"Your granda was no supporter of the British and knew only too well what it meant to be a Catholic in Northern Ireland," Rory said, "but he also realized that violence and guerilla tactics had accomplished nothing to give Catholics a better life up here and, instead, had brought down a storm of heartache and tragedy."

"Such different views must have caused arguments between Granda and his brother," Mick said. "Was there a falling out? Is that why I never heard any of this before?"

"There were hard feelings," Rory said, "but it was what happened with Aiden that broke them up for good. When the IRA regrouped in the mid-1950s, I was not yet ten years old. Aiden would have been about seventeen when the IRA unit led by Seamus Costello came up from the Republic bombing and burning in this area. Aiden was easily recruited after hearing his father's stories all his life. Seamus Costello was about Aiden's age and it must have been exciting to join up with such a young republican leader. They called Costello the 'Boy General' you see. A very enticing figure for a boy like Aiden."

"I found an old newspaper article that listed Aiden, Seamus Costello, and others who were arrested in 1957 when they fled back to the Republic after the raids up here," Cat said. "They were put into MountJoy Prison in Dublin, sentenced to six months there. Instead of being released at the end of that term as they expected, they were interned and moved to the Curragh prison camp in County Kildare. After that, I don't know what became of Aiden. Rory, do you know?"

"I know what my father told me," Rory said. "There was a prison break at the Curragh camp near about Christmas the year after Aiden and Costello and the others were moved there. Aiden was one of the dozen or so men who used wire cutters to get through the fence and make their escape. His friend Costello wasn't among them. I don't know why."

"Did Aiden get away?" Cat asked.

"Yes, he made it out of there and headed north and days later he showed up near here. A local boy brought a note to Aiden's parents to tell them he was back and in hiding nearby. The note asked Aiden's mother go to the Doherty home in Strabane to let Delia know he had returned."

"He was still with my mother?" Cat asked anxiously. "They were still a couple then, even after I was born and she had come back to Strabane? Did he know she left me in New York? Did your father tell you about me . . . about the baby Delia left behind in the States?"

"Take a breath now Caitríona," Rory said. "I will tell you all I know as best I can remember what my father told me. He only talked to me about this in his last years when he was often recalling the past. The rest of what I have to tell you will be hard to hear I'm afraid."

Cat quieted. "Somehow I already know that. I've felt their sorrow for weeks now," she said.

"So, you've some of the fairy in you," Rory said, squeezing Cat's hand.

"Oh, that's for sure," I blurted out.

"Caitríona, there is no doubt that Delia and Aiden were in love," Rory said. "Aiden had worked for Delia's father doing odd jobs since he was in his early teens. He met Delia at the Doherty house and was very taken with her. Her parents were strict and would not permit Aiden (or any young fellow) to take her out as she was not yet eighteen years old. Aiden found ways to see her and before long according to my father, she was sneaking around to be with Aiden. Delia became pregnant with Aiden's child at the age of sixteen or seventeen, a great disgrace for her and an awful heartbreak for her parents. That was when the arrangement was made to send Delia to America to be under the care of my Aunt Sheila."

"That child is you then Caitríona," Mick said. "That means you *are* family to us."

"There is more Caitríona," Rory said. "I believe your mother Delia did mean to bring you home here once she and Aiden were married. Her parents, as you can imagine, blamed Aiden for ruining their daughter and were against any marriage between them. They wanted it to be as if she had never gotten pregnant and forbid her to see Aiden when she returned from America. That was never going to happen. Not long after she came home she turned eighteen and secretly married Aiden who, by that time, had been recruited by Seamus Costello. Her parents, hearing that

Aiden was off with the IRA and suspecting nothing about their marriage, believed they were rid of Aiden and had their daughter back under their rule."

"What went wrong, then?" Cat asked. "They were married, Aiden made it back from the prison camp in Kildare, and his mother was going to tell Delia he was back."

"Aiden was away for a long time and I cannot say if he knew that not long after he fled south with Costello and was arrested, Delia discovered she was once again pregnant. Her parents put her out when she told them she was married to Aiden and carrying his child. She went to live with Aiden's parents and gave birth to a baby boy. If word had gotten to him at Curragh about that, it may have been the reason he later joined the prison break.

"By the time Aiden made it back here, Delia and their baby son, named Patrick, were both very bad with the influenza. After getting Aiden's note, his father sought out his hiding place and brought him home. Delia and the baby were very poorly and soon after Aiden's return they were taken to hospital – the old Strabane Hospital – but it was too late. The influenza took both of them just a week or so after Aiden returned."

"So now I know why my mother never came back for me," Cat said softly. "What happened to Aiden . . . to my father?"

"Aiden had gotten a deep cut from the jagged edge of the metal fence when he broke out of the Curragh prison camp. He paid it no mind, all his thoughts and attention focused on Delia and baby Patrick. Just days after Delia and little Patrick passed on, Aiden awoke to white hot pain and terrible muscle spasms and sweating. The wound was badly infected. He died not long after. My father said it was blood poisoning but I think it must have been tetanus."

Aiden's mother was bereft of any will to live having lost her only child, her baby grandson, and Delia. Her husband Patrick, my uncle, afire with anger, saw his son as a martyr for the republican cause. He went to the Doherty house and raged at Delia's parents. When they said they wanted to bury their daughter, he told them they had abandoned her, that she was an O'Rinn and would be buried with her son . . . and that's what happened. Aiden soon joined them, all three resting together and reunited for eternity. I am sorry to tell you all this Caitríona."

"Well Rory," Cat said, as her tears came, "it's taken sixty years but now I know the truth thanks to you. It's such a sad story but it's my story, my family . . . at last. I do wonder if my O'Rinn or Doherty grandparents ever thought of bringing me home to Ireland after they lost my parents and my baby brother. Did your father ever speak of that?"

Rory sighed. "Actually, I asked my father that question. From what I could get out of him, the Dohertys, blaming Aiden for the ruination and even the death of their daughter, would not have been in a state of mind to bear having a reminder of Aiden in their midst. As for your O'Rinn grandparents, between their overwhelming grief and their meager means, they had little to offer you and, according to my father, were counseled by my Aunt Sheila to leave off the idea of bringing you here to their home. Their understanding was that you had already been adopted and would have a better life in America."

"A *better life*," Cat repeated in a whisper. "Rory, would you know where my parents and brother are buried? I need to go to them."

"I would," Rory said. "My uncle, burning with bitterness, refused to put them in the ground here in Northern Ireland. He bought a plot over in Donegal, at the Murlog Cemetery near St. Patrick's Church in Lifford. That is where they rest as does my uncle and his poor wife."

39. Grave Revelations... Again

We left Rory and Mick on the sidewalk in front of the pub promising to be in touch after visiting the cemetery in Lifford the following day. As an afterthought, Cat had asked Rory if he had any photos of her parents or grandparents. He said he thought not but would look through the old photos he had just in case. Not much was said on the drive back to Strabane. There was too much to take in before it could be talked about. We dropped Eileen off at home and Cat thanked and hugged her for her role in getting Mick to agree to meet. As Cat turned to get back into the car, Eileen called out to her.

"I expect I'll be hearing from the Higgins twins tomorrow. Should they believe that Delia's mother was indeed their own mother's sister, do you still want to go down that road and hear what they have to say?" Eileen asked.

Cat looked down at me and I nodded in a way that told her I thought she should. "Yes, Eileen," Cat called back. "Might as well get both sides of the story. No sense turning back now."

When we got back to the B&B, Maeve met us at the front door. I was sure Eileen had already called her to tell her at least some of what had happed in Castlederg. She said she had a pot of tea on and some warm strawberry rhubarb pie 'just lately out of the oven.' She looked at Cat with such tenderness in her eyes. I marveled at how the Irish can so quickly and sincerely open their hearts to people they hardly know. Cat said she felt she needed to lie down but thanked Maeve for the offer of tea and pie. Maeve, not to be put off, said she would bring up a tray and leave it on the small table in the corner of Cat's bedroom in case she changed her mind.

I was happy to join Maeve in the kitchen for a slice of pie and cup of tea. I hoped she would ask me about the meeting with the O'Rinns. I knew it would do me good to talk about it with her so I could collect my thoughts in anticipation of discussing it with Cat. When she didn't ask, I started the conversation by asking if she had heard from Eileen. Being an honest woman, she said she had received a call from Eileen just before we came back. Eileen told her Cat had found out what became of her parents and it was a sad and tragic story. She asked Maeve to 'take care' of Cat and to 'keep an eye' on me as I would be the one Cat depended on, that being no small burden.

It took three cups of tea and two slices of rhubarb pie to get me through the entire recap of the O'Rinn saga. Maeve let out more than one gasp as I told the story, often patting or squeezing my hands along the way. I had a calming feeling of relief after telling Maeve all of what had happened but I wondered what the next day would bring when the Higgins sisters reported back after talking with their uncle. Should I wish that they found out they were not related to Cat . . . or that they were? Damned if I knew.

Sleep was fitful for both Cat and me that night and, as a result, we were both up, showered, and dressed by seven the next morning. I found Cat in the kitchen having a cup of tea with Maeve when I came down. After a light breakfast, we were off to Lifford, picking up a bouquet of fresh flowers on the way. We were both surprised at the angular, modern facade of the church with its very tall and slim steeple, so different from the other churches we had seen in both Scotland and Ireland. We stopped at the office to get directions to the O'Rinn burial site and, linking our arms for another graveside reckoning, we walked up the path. The monument was modest with a depiction of the Trinity knot at the top and simple engraving of names and dates under the larger lettering "***O'Rinn***:"

Aiden 1938 – 1958   *Patrick 1910 - 1976*

Delia 1939 – 1958   *Caitríona 1914 - 1968*

Patrick 1957 – 1958

"Oh my God," Cat said in amazement, dropping the flowers on the ground. "I was named after my grandmother . . . Aiden's mother."

"The hits just keep coming," I said, shaking my head in disbelief.

As we were walking away from the O'Rinn gravesite, Cat's phone rang. It was Eileen. She asked if we could come over at two that afternoon. The Higgins sisters would be coming too. We said we would be there. Once again picking at our food at lunch, we tried to predict what the Higgins sisters might say. If their Doherty relations and Cat's were one in the same, how would their uncle's account of what happened compare to what Rory O'Rinn had been told by his father? It would be much simpler if their uncle had told them there was no connection between their family and the O'Rinns.

As soon as we walked into Eileen's sitting room and saw Mary and Anna Higgins all atwitter, we knew there was no chance they weren't going to claim kinship with Cat. Eileen intervened saying the tea was on and we should all gather round the table for a snack as we talked. Mary and Anna never took their eyes off Cat as they smiled, grinning from ear-to-ear. As soon as the teapot was put down, Mary jumped right in with her update.

"We rang our Uncle McDaid last evening as we promised," said Mary. "He's a bit of a melter sometimes you see, so we didn't know what to expect. We began by telling him that a question had come up about his sister, our aunt, Fiona Doherty. He asked what kind of *question* had come up and who asked it. I could hear the crankiness coming but I was determined to keep on. I said we had met a visiting American woman who was the daughter of Delia Doherty and we suspected she meant our own cousin Bridget Doherty, called Delia by some."

Anna jumped in at that point to describe how Uncle McDaid reacted to that. "He asked what the *divil* we were about, digging around in such things and, near losing his temper, burst out saying *'her name was Bridget and no one but the O'Rinn boy who ruined her called her Delia'*."

"That did it," said Mary. We knew you were our own cousin, as was your mother."

"But Mary wasn't finished," Anna said, unable to keep silent. "She said we would like to bring you over to Derry to meet him and he should get out the old family pictures to show you your McDaid family."

"What did he say?" asked Cat, trying not to laugh.

"He said we must think that because he's an old man he's an eejit!" Anna said with a girlish giggle. "Then he said he would not have it and hung up on us!"

"Oh Mary and Anna," Cat said. "I am so sorry for getting you in such a fix with your uncle. Will he calm down and get past it?"

"Oh Lord," said Mary, "he already did. He called back this morning as if nothing happened and said we should bring you by at three o'clock this afternoon. He's a strange one."

Cat was game to go see the old man who was no doubt also *her* Uncle McDaid. I drove Cat, Mary, and Anna to Uncle McDaid's apartment in the Bogside section of Derry. He lived walking distance from the Blood Sunday memorial we had visited a few days earlier. Cat had asked Mary and Anna what she could bring Uncle McDaid: something from a bakery, a bottle of whiskey, or even flowers.

"Oh, he loves Clonakilty black pudding," Mary said. "We can stop at Dunnes and get some."

Cat and I both made a disgusted face in response to the words *black pudding*. "Mary," Cat asked, "will he want to serve it to us when we are visiting him? Nicola and I haven't quite developed a taste for Irish pudding – black or white."

"No, no, dear," Mary said. "He won't. He may offer us a bun and some tea but he'll save the Clonakilty all for himself. Our mother used to say the McDaids must have some Scottish blood in them, the men being so frugal . . . and so it is with Uncle McDaid."

40. Pictures & a Thousand More Words

"Well," Uncle McDaid said, "let's get a look at ya. Step over here by the window where there's more light. So you say you are Bridget Doherty's child come all the way from America after all these years."

"Yes, Mr. McDaid," Cat said, "that's exactly what I'm saying. Thank you for having me to your home."

"And just who is this girlie over here?" he asked, focusing his narrow-eyed gaze on Nicola. "Another one of Bridget's daughters?"

Cat, realizing Uncle McDaid the 'melter' had returned, smiled sweetly. "No, Mr. McDaid, she is my dearest friend. Her name is Nicola. Oh, I almost forgot, we brought you a little something to thank you for having us to your home," she said, handing him the package of Clonakilty pudding.

He opened the wrapping and a sly smile came over his face as he turned in the direction of his nieces. "I expect I can use this," he said and disappeared into his small kitchen where he no doubt put it safely into the fridge.

As predicted, he eventually offered tea and buns to his guests, no mention of the pudding. Cat asked if he would like to hear more about her and how she came to believe that Bridget Doherty was her mother. She wisely left out the name of her father when telling the tale. No sense to poke the melter. (Eileen explained later that a *melter* means an annoying person. Check.)

Uncle McDaid's version of the Doherty-O'Rinn story was, all things considered, not much different than Rory's: an impressionable young girl immorally drawn away from her family by a young boy raised 'loosely,' his head filled with romanticized tales of republican exploits. He never spoke Aiden's name or the word love in talking about them nor did he mention their marriage. He did say Bridget's death gutted her mother (his sister Fiona) and all but sent her to her grave right there and then. He made mention of Bridget's parents being refused the right to take care of her burial arrangements, calling that 'a despicable thing.'

That said, he walked over to a corner cabinet, opened the double doors and took out what had to be an old photo album with a time-worn cover. He plopped it on the table, opened it, and started showing us the photos, pointing out people and occasions captured by the camera. Most of the photos were old black and whites held on the black album pages with small paper corners. I could see Cat trying to take it all in. I pulled a small notebook and pen out of my purse and start taking notes. I wondered how the hell we could get Uncle McDaid to let us borrow any of the photos that included Cat's mother or her Doherty grandparents so we could have copies made before we left for home.

He stopped suddenly on one page. "There she is, our Bridget," he said, "standing next to her parents – you'd be calling them your own grandparents I expect. My sister Fiona was so lovely when she was young – handsome even when she was older – until Bridget died. She was only half-alive after that."

Anna leaned in to get a closer look. "Uncle, you must see the resemblance between Aunt Fiona and Caitríona here. You see it don't you Mary?"

"Aye," Mary said, "I do indeed."

"None of our people have red hair like this one," Uncle McDaid said gesturing in Cat's direction. "That must be from the O'Rinn side."

"Actually," Cat said with a smirk, "it's from the Clairol people."

I gave Cat a quick kick in the shin under the table accompanied by my best menacing look.

"Clare?" Uncle McDaid said, screwing up his face. "We have no family from Clare."

Mary and Anna, enjoying the situation and fully understanding what Cat was about, pursed their lips trying not to laugh.

"Uncle," Mary said. "Caitríona is pulling your leg . . . just a bit of fun. The word is C-L-A-I-R-O-L. It's a ladies' hair dye. It's her way of telling you you're not seeing the natural color of her hair."

"In fact, truth be told," Cat said, "I'm nearly as gray as you, Mr. McDaid."

Uncle McDaid pondered that for a minute and then returned to his narrative of the photos in the old album. There were several photos that included Cat's mother or Cat's grandparents. I pulled out my phone and moved closer. Without asking, I squeezed in as close as I could and began snapping photos of the album photos. Uncle McDaid lurched back and I prepared to be 'melted.'

"What malarkey is this Missy?" scolded Uncle McDaid. "Where's your manners?"

"Begging your pardon, Mr. McDaid," I said. "I know these photos are precious to you and dared not ask that you let us take them to have copies made for Caitríona. She has not one picture of either of her parents or any of her grandparents you understand. I thought I would try to take photos of your pictures so she would have something to remember her mother and grandparents."

A silence fell over the room as everyone waited for Uncle McDaid to speak. He narrowed his eyes and his gaze lingered on me. I tried to channel Bambi, big brown eyes opened wide and a vulnerable look on my face. He inhaled (bigtime) and I braced for whatever was coming. Arms folded across his chest, he exhaled and parted his thin lips.

"Very thoughtful aren't you Missy?" he said, a wry smile coming over his ruddy wrinkled face. "Next time ask me first . . . but, considering how things are for your friend, I would let you borrow a few of the photos as long as you bring them back tomorrow and, on the way, you might get some more of that pudding."

The Higgins sisters appeared a bit pained and embarrassed by their uncle's antics but wasted no time stepping up and carefully removing the photos we needed to have copied. The four of us beat a hasty retreat before Uncle McDaid had another mood-swing.

Uncle McDaid was a wily old fox. He played us like a drum. Cat and I agreed he was an irresistible force of nature and just plain loveable, the official curmudgeon of her new Irish family.

41. Family Reunions

The first order of business the following morning was to get the photos copied and then go to Dunnes for another package of Clonakilty pudding. Before noon we were at Uncle McDaid's. We knocked, the door opened and, without an invitation to come inside, he reached out to take his photos and the precious pudding, giving a quick nod as he closed the door. I imagined him shuffling into the kitchen with the pudding, delighted at his coup.

As I drove us back toward Strabane, Cat phoned Mick O'Rinn to update him on the McDaid-Doherty connection. He said he would call his father right away to give him the news and would ask if he found any old family photos Cat should see. About an hour later, not long after we got back to the B&B, Mick called. His father was organizing an impromptu family reunion over in Castlederg and wanted to be sure we would be free to come. Mick handed his phone to Rory and Cat put him on speaker.

"Ladies," Rory said, "do you know what Ireland's own George Bernard Shaw once said about families?"

"No we don't," Cat said, "but I guess you're going to tell us."

Rory chuckled. "Shaw said that if you cannot get rid of a family skeleton, you may as well make it dance. That's what we're going to do – air it all out to music with a family reunion tomorrow afternoon at the pub where we met the other day. Invite Eileen and those Higgins sisters. Hell, invite old man McDaid if you want."

Mick took back the phone. "I have never seen my father like this in my life. This thing with Aiden O'Rinn has changed him. He seems happier than he has been in a long time. It's all your doing. My daughter Siobhan is so anxious to meet you and Nicola. See what you started?"

"Well," Cat said, "we have two more days here before we leave for home so let it be a family reunion and going away party all-in-one. We'll invite Eileen, the Higgins sisters, and Maeve, our B&B host who got the ball rolling by introducing us to Eileen. As for my new McDaid great-uncle, I know he's not ready to be surrounded by O'Rinns . . . not yet anyway. See you all tomorrow!"

When Cat and I went out for dinner that evening our appetites returned with a vengeance. We started with shrimp cocktail with Marie Rose sauce and mussels in white wine with crusty bread, followed that with an entree of local seafood, and ended our feast with more of that strawberry rhubarb pie. It felt good to be hungry again.

Rory's family reunion kicked off in the pub's lounge at two and since it was Saturday and word had spread about the new American O'Rinn, the place was already jumping when we arrived with Eileen, Maeve, and the Higgins sisters. It was a bit overwhelming and, for a minute or two, we hovered in the doorway looking for Rory or Mick. Before we spotted them, a beautiful young woman with wavy copper-streaked brown hair made a beeline in our direction.

"Caitríona?" she asked, trying to figure out who was who. "I'm Siobhan O'Rinn . . . Mick is my father."

Cat stepped forward and stuck out her hand. Siobhan responded with a vigorous hug. Ice broken, Cat introduced the rest of us and we followed Siobhan who delivered us to Mick and Rory. Mick offered to get us drinks and Rory told us what he had planned. Live music would be starting in a half-hour but first proper introductions had to be made. Rory stepped up to the standing microphone that had been set up for the musicians and gave a shout-out to the crowd to get their attention.

"Friends," he said, "and the rest of you freeloaders, I'd like to introduce you to an American woman so daft she came three-thousand miles with the purpose of convincing us that she belonged in our clan. Imagine that, someone that wants to be an

O'Rinn! You know what they say about Irish-Americans and their determination to reconnect with their roots. Well, by God, it's true, here's the living proof: my own cousin Caitríona, the granddaughter of my own uncle Patrick O'Rinn, God rest his soul."

Rory was forced to pause as glasses were raised and cheers rang out for the newest member of the O'Rinn clan. As soon as the crowd quieted a bit, he leaned into the microphone and started up again.

"Our Caitríona has brought her new-found cousins from her mother's side with her today. Please welcome the lovely Higgins sisters, Mary and Anna. Their auntie was Caitríona's grandmother McDaid who married a Doherty over in Strabane. In a matter of mere days, Caitríona has managed to get the O'Rinns and McDaids to bare their souls about family and feelings not spoken of for ages. She says we have given her back her family but, truth be told, she has done more for us than we did for her. Get over here Caitríona and say a few words to explain yourself."

Cat, a combination of tears and fear, joined Rory at the microphone. She had a shy look on her face that was like nothing I had ever seen in the ten years I knew her. She moved close to the microphone, cleared her throat and began.

"I don't know how to tell you how happy I am to be here, to have a family and to finally know who I am – the best part being that I'm Irish. Holy shit, I'm really Irish!"

That provoked more cheers, more raised glasses, and a good deal of warm-hearted laughing. I saw Mary and Anna Higgins cheering with delight. Rory looked as proud as the proverbial peacock and Siobhan was jumping up and down and hugging her father Mick.

"Everyone, I want you to meet the women who made this possible," Cat said, motioning for me, Eileen, and Maeve to join her. "Please say hi to my best friend Nicola who has been with me every step of the way as I searched for my family – from New York to Ireland - and to Eileen and Maeve, our new Irish friends who connected us with Mick and Rory. I still cannot believe we unraveled the mystery of my birth and found my family."

Rory stepped up, announced that the music was about to start and told everyone to enjoy themselves. Even though it was Cat's party, I had the best time of my life – everyone did. We danced, sang, drank, and ate in a whirl of best wishes from new family and friends. By five o'clock, things started winding down and we thought we would be heading off to Strabane to drop off Eileen and the Higgins sisters, then going on to Maeve's. We were wrong. Rory had other plans for us.

"Girls," he said with a wide grin, "we'll be having dinner now at Mick's, followed by a private party for just ourselves . . . and one other guest. Let's be going over to Mick's now. He and Siobhan are waiting for us and the lamb shanks are ready to be dished out."

The long wooden farm table was set for ten and the aroma of slow-cooked braised lamb filled Mick and Siobhan's small cozy home. Before I could get to wondering who guest number ten was, there was a knock at the door. Mick went to the door and welcomed a man I guessed to be in his eighties. As he shook Mick's hand, he removed his tweed cap and nodded to the rest of us. His full thick head of white hair curled around and over his ears and covered the back of his neck, turning up at his collar. He was small-framed and not more than a couple inches over five feet tall. The stem of a pipe stuck up from the pocket of his vest and I imagined he had a pouch of tobacco tucked inside it somewhere. I saw Cat giving him a similar once-over. I hoped I was more subtle than she was as she studied him.

"Girls," Rory said, walking up and shaking the man's hand. "May I introduce Paddy Sullivan, one of the last seanchaithe in these parts. I invited Paddy to pass the evening with us. Paddy, mo chara, many thanks for coming."

Turning to Cat, he continued. "Caitriona, I know you have a lot of questions about the days when your parents were young. Paddy is the man to tell you tales of life in those days. I can promise you that not only will he be able to answer some of your questions, he

Maureen K. Wlodarczyk

will all but transport you back there with his storytelling. But first, let's eat that lovely lamb."

"Everyone, please be seated," said Siobhan. "We've potatoes, turnips and carrots along with the 'lovely' lamb. Leave some room for dessert – Cat's favorite – strawberry rhubarb pie."

42. Mid-Century Meanderings

The meal was scrumptious. Cat and I helped clear, wash, and dry the dishes after dinner and dessert, sending everyone else to the parlor for an after-dinner drink of Jameson's or Bailey's. Working under Siobhan's direction, we were done in no time and soon joined the others. Mick had lit a turf fire in the hearth and Paddy Sullivan was seated in a stuffed chair alongside the fire where he looked quite at home as he puffed on his pipe. Cat poured herself some Bailey's and took a seat on the sofa next to me. Paddy Sullivan downed the last swallow of his whiskey and made eye contact with Cat.

"Caitríona," he said, "Rory's told me you only recently discovered you were adopted and set out to find your birth family, that search bringing you here. I'm told that yer Da was Aiden O'Rinn, a young boy from this very place who joined up with the IRA during the Border Campaign. I'm from up the road in Derry meself, born in Bogside. I was a young married man in my twenties and my wife was expecting our first child at the time that IRA operation came on. Like most folks my age, recalling what went on in the old days is more easily done than trying to remember what happened a month or two ago. All these years later it's still grand to tell the old stories. So, Caitríona, how should we start?"

I watched Cat, hoping she would open up and ask at least some of the questions percolating in her brain. I bit down on my lower lip to remind myself that, just because she had told me the questions that were dogging her, I had no right to interfere. Some of those questions were contextual and benign enough. *What was it like growing up in Ireland for those born just a decade or so after the birth of the Irish Free State? What was it like for the Irish population in the aftermath of the partitioning of the island and the bloody civil war that followed? Did people come together or did the bitter divisions among former brothers-in-arms taint the two decades that followed?*

Cat had immersed herself in researching the early decades following Irish independence and was well-informed when it came to what books and newspaper accounts had to offer on the subject. Paddy Sullivan offered the chance to hear personal recollections and ask questions of someone who had lived where her parents had lived, when they had been growing up there. He seemed just the person to give Cat the kind of context she was looking for in a way

Birthless

that no book or newspaper story could. While names and dates on a family tree chart are helpful in understanding where a person comes from, it takes context to turn those facts into the actual life story of one's ancestors.

Beyond the kinds of questions bouncing around in Cat's head that Paddy could likely answer, she was jousting with other questions and thoughts, the ones that could not be resolved by applying facts, logic or context. The most troubling were the thoughts about her father Aiden's life as an IRA guerrilla. Just the night before, as we had a late night cup of tea at Maeve's, Cat had talked about struggling with conflicting feelings about her father's IRA involvement.

"Nic," she had said, "the IRA killed people and apparently had no remorse about it, especially when the dead were police or politicians supporting the partitioning of the island and continuing ties to England. Innocent people on both sides were hurt or killed in the cross-fire. I know that Catholics in Northern Ireland were treated very badly by the authorities, held down by active religious prejudice and denied the rights and opportunities of their Protestant neighbors. How long can people be expected to endure that . . . but is violence ever the right answer?

"I am convinced of one thing," she continued. "The British practiced religious persecution for centuries and used the carrot and stick method to get people to convert. More than that, they

245

fostered the widely-held belief that the conflict in Northern Ireland was about religion when the truth was (and is) that the friction and bitterness is rooted in institutionalized economic and social inequality."

"Well," I had said in response to that earful, "I don't know about you but I'm getting a little hot under the collar just listening to what you're saying. Not hard to imagine how we would have felt if we were living with that institutionalized inequality, is it? It just isn't possible to walk in your father's shoes and objectively compile a list of pros and cons related to the decisions he made. Maybe you just have to give him the benefit of the doubt and let it go, especially considering he was a teenager when he joined up."

I don't know how long I was off reliving that conversation from the prior night but my mind was called back when I heard Cat's voice.

"Mr. Sullivan," she said, "are you a Catholic?"

Of all the questions I thought she might ask him, that wasn't one of them.

"I am," Paddy said. "Why do you ask?"

"Well," she said, "since my parents were Catholics it seems to me that hearing about life here when they were young would be more meaningful and on-point if the person telling me about it had a frame of reference similar to theirs."

"A very logical surmise," he said, taking a puff on his pipe.

"So, what was it like growing up here in the 1940s and 50s?" Cat asked.

"Are you familiar with the so-called 'Celtic Tiger' of the 1990s and early 21st century?" said Paddy.

"Of course," Cat said.

"It was the opposite of that," Paddy said, "both up here and in the Republic. It was actually worse down there. Remember that the Republic was a new state trying to find its way to a future. It was a bit like a blind man trying to feel his way forward or a baby trying to learn to walk. Some pundits described it as the worst time since the Great Famine. By the 1950s Ireland was bleeding emigrants as people simply gave up the struggle and left away from here.

"In Northern Ireland, in the 1940s, there was once again some nationalist activity – not the IRA or anything violent – but enough organization to cause the government concern. It was going on at the time the Free State took the final steps to leave the British Commonwealth and officially become the Republic of Ireland. Nationalist sentiments up here cooled when some social welfare programs were put in place that actually helped improve life a bit for many of the poor. Just the same, there was persistent discrimination against Catholics when it came to housing and jobs. A Catholic underclass without opportunities or hope would prove fertile ground for the civil rights movement that rose up in in the 1960s. There's only so long that people will live under a system based on inequality before they turn on those that enforce it. The pity is that the means of getting out from under so often comes with violence and bloodshed."

"Do you have any recollections about the IRA Border Campaign and things that happened up here?" Cat asked.

"Some," he said, "but nothing about your own father. It was a time when the IRA was trying to rebuild itself after all but ceasing to exist in the decade before that. Men who had fought shoulder-to-shoulder during the war for independence fell out in a most bitter and often violent way over the treaty that partitioned the island and left the six counties up here under the British flag. The bloody civil war that followed left deep scars and vendettas in its wake and there was no reconciliation or healing. The IRA was outlaw to the governments on both sides of the border, further weakening the organization.

"In the late 1940s, there was a revival of sorts, the first order of business being operations to recruit and rearm in preparation for guerrilla attacks up here. After some success with rearming, a plan was hatched to use the so-called 'flying column' method for strikes across the border from the Republic into the North."

"I read about some of the IRA attacks near here," Cat said, "the burning of the Magherafelt courthouse, bombings at police barracks and at the BBC building in Derry. I believe my father was involved in the burning at Magherafelt under Seamus Costello."

"Ah," said Paddy, "the famous Boy General from Wicklow. There were also smaller incidents right in this area . . . in Omagh, Strabane, and even one here in Castlederg. I recall the bombing of government offices in Strabane, a customs office and a labor agency I believe. The truth is that the Border Campaign, never very successful, limped on with sporadic activity until the early 1960s when they finally gave it up. You'll have to dig hard to find anyone, friend or foe of the IRA, that will call it anything but a failed operation.

"What no one foresaw was that, just several years later, Northern Ireland would be turned on its head for decades by the Troubles. When I think of all those who died, my heart hurts. My oldest son was there on Bloody Sunday. Just fifteen, he wanted to watch the march for Catholic civil rights. My wife and I told him, reluctantly, that he could go but forbid him to join in the march. When the shooting started and panic set in, he ran for home and, thank God, was unhurt. If he had been one of those cut down that day by the British paratroopers, I have no doubt that I would have wanted an eye for an eye. I have the greatest admiration for the families of the dead and wounded that persisted for nearly forty years to restore the good names of their own and make the British finally admit that what happened was nothing else but murder."

Paddy paused and closed his eyes for a few seconds. I wondered if he was trying to shake off the images of Bloody Sunday that had come back to him as he talked about that day. When he reopened his eyes, he smiled in Cat's direction.

"Well Caitríona, I expect I've added a good bit more commentary than I should have in answer to your questions."

"Not at all Mr. Sullivan," Cat said. "I thank you for sharing all of it with us, especially with me. Honestly, I've been struggling with many mixed feelings about my father's involvement in the IRA. Nicola reminded me that I can't walk in his shoes and I know I can't judge him from a distance of over fifty years and three thousand miles of ocean."

"I expect we can all agree with the wisdom of that Caitríona," Paddy said. "Ach, I see Siobhan has gone off to the kitchen, no doubt to wet the tea. Before we partake, I would like to tell you about a connection between your mother's home place, Strabane, and the birth of America. It was a Strabane man, John Dunlap, who printed the first copies of your Declaration of Independence. He left here to apprentice in his uncle's print shop in Philadelphia and then took it over from the uncle. More than that, he fought in your American Revolution with George Washington. Imagine that!"

Siobhan set out the tea with some cakes and, our bellies full and warm, a long and somewhat exhausting day came to an end.

43. Frozen in Time

On our last day before leaving for the airport in Belfast, we went back to the Murlog Cemetery one more time. I promised Cat she would be back. . . . I knew she would. After that we went to Rory's to say goodbye. Mick and Siobhan were there. Siobhan gave Cat an envelope of photos, each neatly labeled on the reverse to identify those in the picture, the occasion, and the approximate date the photo was taken. She had gone through the photos with her grandfather Rory, had copies made, and did the labeling herself. Cat hugged her and said she would go through them, magnifying glass in hand, once we got home.

I saw the way Cat looked at her. Siobhan was the same age Gemma was when she died. Like Gemma, Siobhan was brimming over with the enthusiasm and anticipation of youth. She told us she would graduate at the end of this school year and would then

251

go on to study at Ulster University. She planned to get a degree in history and was already talking about applying for internships with PRONI (the Public Record Office of Northern Ireland) and the OPW (public works preservation organization) in the Republic. She was a gem!

Phone numbers, email addresses, and postal addresses were exchanged with the O'Rinns, the Higgins sisters, Eileen and Maeve. Many, many group and individual photos were taken. The goodbyes came with laughing, tears, hugs, kisses, and promises for the future. When we fell into our seats in first class for the flight home, we had not an iota of strength left. I'd like to say we took advantage of the situation to get some sleep and recharge ourselves but we were too wired and too chatty for that to happen. Just as well. Dozing off would have meant missing the flight attendant's offer to make us customized ice cream sundaes. Not an option.

When we got home and unpacked we found we had accumulated something close to a lifetime supply of Scottish and Irish wool scarves, hats, and gloves. We decided we would bring a box of assorted items to Sister Cecilia for the nuns and also take some things over to Sunrise. There was good news in the pile of mail waiting for us when we got back: invitations to attend Ellen and Mateo's wedding.

The first order of business after unpacking and picking through our mail was to open a bottle of wine and look through the envelope of photos Siobhan had given Cat along with the photos from Uncle McDaid's album that we had copied. For people our age, there is something nostalgic and sometimes sad about looking at old black and white snapshots. When my father and then my mother died, I was the one who cleaned out their home and put it up for sale. Sam helped me with the heavy lifting as we prepared furniture donations for The Salvation Army and packed boxes of household items and bags of clothes for St. Vincent de Paul. I was glad my parents had a modest home and weren't inclined to accumulate *things*. The part no one else but me could do was the hardest: going through the personal effects that had no tangible value but were so evocative of my parents and their daily lives . . . and so potent in bringing back memories. Rosary beads, Timex watches, old costume jewelry not worn in decades, favorite books, dozens of old funeral cards in a dresser drawer, my mother's address book, scraps of paper with recipes, and albums and boxes of photos spanning at least a half-century.

I went through all those photos, sorting them into piles. Besides those I kept for myself, I put together packages of pictures of my cousins and their parents taken when we were children and sent those on to each of them. I tried hard to find every photo a new home but, left with a pile of photos of people I could not remember or identify, I had to give in and decide how to dispose of them. I could have tossed them in the recycling bin or the trash but something made me uncomfortable doing that – it was just too impersonal. Instead I decided to 'cremate' them, reducing them to unidentifiable wisps of paper 'ashes' with my shredder.

In Cat's case, there were only about twenty photos and all were keepers. We spread them out on the kitchen table. I took out the notes I had taken down when Uncle McDaid had been explaining the photos in his album and we labeled the reverse of the half-dozen photos of his that we had copied in Derry. With all the photos identified, we started taking a closer look at them one-by-one, eyeglasses and magnifying glasses at the ready.

We looked at the faces, their varied expressions sometimes readable, other times not. The camera had captured happiness communicated by wide smiles and eyes crinkled by uplifted cheeks. Those had us smiling right back involuntarily. Other shots caught people in their (modest) Sunday best, some suggesting a family gathered for a funeral and others a more festive occasion. We took time to study the backgrounds as well as the people in the photos: cottages, signs of farming activity, old stone churches, street and countryside views.

I thought Cat would all but transport herself into the photos of her parents and grandparents, O'Rinns and Dohertys both. If sheer will could have allowed her to time travel, she would have done it. Her eyes lingered on those precious photos, drinking them in like a parched desert wanderer who discovered a trickle of water. The most powerful of the photos was the saddest: Cat's mother Delia

Birthless

sitting in a wooden rocker, a quilt wrapped around her and baby Patrick on her lap. Cat's father Aiden is crouched down beside her. Delia, a faint smile on her face, looks so very frail. Aiden's hand covers hers. His smile seems reluctant, a struggle between hopefulness and despair. Little Patrick, about a year old, lays his weary head on his mother's breast. Their faces telegraph their anguish and foreshadow their short-lived reunion.

I scanned all the photos for Cat and she had a second set of physical copies made . . . just in case. After that, over the next few weeks, we went through the hundreds of photos we took in Scotland and Ireland. That process was marked by much laughing and much wine consumption and we found we were missing the people and places we had left behind. Cat was already planning to invite Siobhan to visit the next summer after she graduated and she asked me if I thought Mary and Anna Higgins were up to making the trip to see us as well.

"I, myself, sorely miss Uncle McDaid," I said smirking. "If the twins come, they must bring him with them . . . before the old boy falls off his perch."

"Well, *Missy*," Cat said drily, "no way he'll come without a Clonakilty pudding bribe being part of the plan. Good luck finding some of that stuff around here."

We raised and drained our wine glasses in salute to Uncle McDaid.

"I do wish we had brought a DNA kit to his apartment," I said.

255

"Can you imagine talking him into spitting in a tube? Just picture it."

"I don't think there's enough Clonakilty pudding in all of Ireland to get him to do that," Cat said with a big grin.

Epilogue:
Nicola

Cat and I went from being a family of two to something quite different from that point on. We now had connections in Louisiana, Ireland, and Scotland, a global network of family and friends. We were suddenly interested in getting on Skype and setting up international calling plans on our phones. We had new birthdays to add to our card lists. St. Patrick's Day took on a new significance, and Hogmanay became our newest celebration.

We made it to Ellen's wedding. If there could be a cure for my and Cat's tendency to jadedness when it came to marriage, Ellen and Mateo were it. They were also the poster children for fairytale happy endings. It was a perfect, joy-filled day.

Siobhan graduated and Rory bought her a round-trip plane ticket to New York. After planning her month-long stay with Cat, she suggested that perhaps she could ask Mary and Anna Higgins to come to New York for a short stay at the same time. Cat asked me what I thought. I was more than game and, between the two of us, we had plenty of room for all three of them. They arrived together, same flight from Belfast to LaGuardia.

Honest to God, having the Higgins twins with us for ten days was a blast. Those two girls were a delight, up for almost anything. The most memorable of their American adventures involved spitting in a plastic tube. Yes, Cat ordered DNA test kits, one for Siobhan and the other for either of the Higgins sisters. Much animated conversation took place as Mary and Anna discussed (debated) which of them would do the spitting. In the end, Anna deferred (as usual) and settled for cheering Mary on. The whole episode, from spirited debating to enthusiastic spitting, had all the elements of a video that would have gone viral if posted on-line. As expected, when the test results came back, there was absolute confirmation that Cat was a cousin to both Siobhan and the Higgins sisters.

Cat reveled in her time with Siobhan. It seemed a perfect pairing of two kindred souls. Cat had lost her only child and Siobhan had lost her mother eight years earlier to breast cancer. They fit together like two perfectly cut puzzle pieces, one extending out to fill the gap in the other. There was no doubt in my mind that they would grow closer as time went by.

And then there was me . . . and Alec Campbell. When I got home from Ireland, there was a letter waiting for me from Alec. It was warm but a bit restrained, a sign of his desire not to overstep the bounds of our new acquaintance I believed. I like old-fashioned ways of communicating: paper invitations, hand-written thank-you cards, and lines of script on personal stationery. Although we talked via Skype or on the phone and did email and text, we kept corresponding using postal mail. Unlike Cat and Siobhan, we weren't embarking on a brand new relationship with a clean slate and great expectations. We had history - translate that *baggage* - and had to rebuild the road that could bring us together. Plus, we needed to get to know each other in a way that our past brief encounter hadn't allowed. I know Alec would have come to New York for a visit if I had asked him but I chose to go to Edinburgh instead so I would be able to visit Duncan once again.

About ten days before I was to leave for Edinburgh, Cat and I had plans for dinner. She called to beg off less than an hour before I was supposed to pick her up saying she wasn't feeling well. I asked what was wrong.

"I feel like I have something dead in my stomach," she said. "I've been feeling nauseous for a couple days and just a little while ago I threw up three times, even after I was sure there was nothing left in my stomach. Oh shit, I'm going to retch again."

She dropped the phone. I grabbed my car keys and headed for her house as fast as I could. I let myself in and yelled for her. I heard her moaning and followed the sound into her master bathroom. She was on her knees gripping the toilet seat, doubled over in pain. "Nic," she cried. "The pain, the pain is like a hot knife burning through me and it's getting sharper."

I hooked my arms under her arm pits, heaved her up and got her onto her bed and then I called 911. The ambulance came in minutes. I told them what I could about Cat's symptoms as she was writhing in such terrible pain she couldn't answer their questions. I followed the paramedics to the hospital.

As I sat at the desk in the admitting department answering questions about Cat and filling out forms once again, I remembered the night eighteen months before when Cat took a flier on the ice. So much had happened and changed since then. Reaching into Cat's tote bag to get out her insurance card, I spotted a small zipper bag. I just had to open it to see if she was still carrying around a clean pair of drawers . . . just in case. Yep, she was.

When I got back to the ER, the nurse told me Cat had been given something for pain but was still in a bad way. Blood had been drawn and sent to the lab. While it might be gastroenteritis, Cat was going to be taken for a scan of her abdomen 'soon' to determine if there was something else going on. *Soon* turned out to be four hours and most of that time Cat was still in a good deal of pain. I sat at her bedside feeling helpless and getting more pissed off by the hour.

The scan results finally came back: appendicitis. The ER doctor told Cat she had an 'unusually long appendix' that had to be removed pronto. I knew the pain meds were having their effect by her response.

"Shit. Surgery? Well then, maybe you can put that big old appendix of mine in a jar and send it to Ripley's Believe It Or Not or submit it to the Guinness Book of World Records."

Sometimes now, watching Cat take someone to task, I swear she has more than a bit of her Uncle McDaid in her. The doctor quickly escaped through the curtain surrounding Cat's bed and a nurse came in with paperwork to be filled out, including a new advance directive form, the old form no longer in use she said. Cat called the nurse back, waving the advance directive form.

"We'll need another one of these," she said winking at me. "It's still you for me and me for you Nic."

She was right. Some things hadn't changed.

~~~~~~~~~~~~~~~~~~~~~~~~~~~~~~~~~~

In Memory of My Mother Arlene

Made in the USA
Charleston, SC
26 August 2016